CW01583106

John Hodge

THE FAT CLUB

Limited Special Edition. No. 2 of 25 Paperbacks

The author is a person who has always had an imagination, starting at an early age and throughout his life. Now he is in his 60s and he has decided to put his imagination into words and so it starts again, in the form of a book called *The Fat Club*. It's not what it seems.

John Hodge

THE FAT CLUB

AUSTIN MACAULEY PUBLISHERS™
LONDON • CAMBRIDGE • NEW YORK • SHARJAH

A CIP catalogue record for this title is available from the British Library.

ISBN 9781528932509 (Paperback)
ISBN 9781528967099 (ePub e-book)

www.austinmacauley.com

First Published (2019)
Austin Macauley Publishers Ltd
25 Canada Square
Canary Wharf
London
E14 5LQ

I'd like to acknowledge my wife, Yvette, who has always been at my side in everything I've done and always steered me down the right path, so it was no surprise when I told her the story about the fat club and she said, "Why don't you write a book?" and again, she's been with me every step of the way. Thank you, Chicken.

Chapter 1

The flight was long and tedious back from St Lucia, they were both on their second on board flight film when Summer took off her headphones and said to Simon, "Wasn't Coconut Bay lovely?" The bay was set in 85 acres and it was a place you could easily get lost in, the palm trees lined the sandy beach like soldiers on Parade, and the food and drink was to die for, and there in lied the problem, they had both put on a few pounds, but they were both fitness fanatics and knew the weight would soon drop off. For Simon, it was an easy task, he had his own gym and used it every day without fail. He would scour the Internet for supplements and any quick fix he could get his hands on. His body was chiselled but not too over the top and even though it wasn't hard for him to keep in shape, he was now hitting sixty, but people still put him in his late forties. Summer, on the other hand, had a great body but had to work really hard to keep it in shape. She would constantly go off track and then have to work even harder to get it back off.

They were now on the last leg of the flight home. Simon knew this because the third and last film had just started. He turned to Summer as she was just about to nod off, "It's the third film, Summer. We're nearly home weather permitting." Summer looked at him, her look was enough. Two hours later, the airbus A330 was now descending over the UK, and Summer had just woke up. She was now even more fidgety then she was before, eight hours flying was enough for anybody, especially when you were flying back home. The plane moved from side to side as it flew through the clouds.

Simon looked down, "There's Gatwick, won't be long now." They both got home four hours later after long delays in the airport, the taxi driver pulled up on their driveway. Simon knew the driver, it was his good friend, Tony.

"So how's business been, mate? Have I missed anything?"

Simon had his own business, he was a chauffeur and had a high-end £64,000 car bought with a loan from the bank; he was basically a high-end taxi driver and had a good healthy work diary.

"Yes, mate, it's been quite busy but still nowhere near your league."

Summer asked how his family was. "They're fine," he said as he popped the boot open. Simon took some money from his pocket. "Put your money away, mate, you know it's not about that. You would do the same for me. The headlights of Tony's car danced across the main wall of the living room as he reversed off the drive and drove off down the avenue.

At last, they were both home. "St Lucia is a lovely place but it's a pain getting there and back," said Summer as she dropped back into her chair and kicked off her shoes. The time was now one am Saturday morning, and they both knew they still had about 8 hours of jet lag to get over. Summer worked for the NHS as an occupational therapist and wasn't back at work till Monday morning but for Simon, it was different. He had a job booked in for Saturday afternoon, his holiday was now over, there was money to be made, so jet lag or no jet lag, he had to get some sleep.

Saturday, nine am, soon came around. It only felt like Simon had just touched his pillowcase with his now somewhat tired head, when that awful unpleasant sound of his alarm clock set off, that sound of the cheesy Melody from his phone, that for some reason was called daffodils in the forest, but then he thought, *It's better than listening to walking on snow tops, now that is cheesy.*

Summer pushed him in the back, as if he wasn't hurting enough from his jet lag. "Are you going to turn that noise off, and go back to sleep or are you getting up? Either way, make up your mind and turn it off." His mind was made up. Although Summer was beautiful in his eyes, she snored like a weather balloon that had a small hole in it, and rather than asking Summer to turnover, which he thought better of, made his move and got out of bed. It was as if he had been taking sleeping tablets, he couldn't open his eyes. He was walking into walls, the feel of different types of carpet from the bedroom to the landing led him the way. He managed to get down stairs without breaking any of his toes, this was only because he had broken one before and now knew better. Now Simon was safely at the bottom of the stairs, he checked his central heating thermostat, fourteen Celsius, he tapped the glass, everything was good. He had set the heating to acclimatise himself to the weather back home only because of the difference in heat back in St Lucia.

He then made his way into the kitchen where his pride and joy was sitting on the worktop waiting for him, his coffee making machine. He took out a filter from the cupboard and then put four scoops of coffee into the filter then added water, and then sat down and just listened to his machine doing its work. Now he knew he was back home, it was done, his coffee was ready. He poured a nice hot cup and then sat at the island in the kitchen turning on his iPad to check his emails, two hundred and five emails. Checking down the list, a lot of them were spams and they went straight into the bin. "Thank God," he said to himself. Time was getting on and he knew he had to get a move on, he was picking up his customer at sixteen hundred hours. He had a quick shower, then tiptoed passed the main bedroom into the dressing room so not to wake up Summer. The wardrobe doors opened with a movement sensor that he had fitted on to the front of the doors. He was mad on his gadgets and anything he could do to save a bit of time was good by him. He pulled out what he called his work uniform, black pants, black shoes, white shirt and a black tie, all was good as he looked in the mirror one last time before putting his favourite aftershave on. His coffee machine bleeped again as he walked down the hallway to the front door. "Maybe just one more cup," he said to himself, and as he balanced his coffee and his mail from the last two weeks, he still managed to open his front door and then walked down his path to the garage pushing the fob that was in his pocket. It was like Sinbad saying open sesame, then the garage door began to lift open. As part of his bank loan, he had a garage extension big enough to get his car in and have his office at the back. Summer had fallen out with him a number of times over the fact that the house was overrun with Simon's work and it didn't feel like their home anymore. But all was well now, the house was Summer's again with expensive floor coverings and all the trimmings that met with her taste, and Simon was the one who put the time into pay for it, but what did he care, he had his own den, his cave, his beloved garage. The smell of leather upholstery filled the air as the garage door lifted up as the lights came on with a light sensor. This was the hub of Simon's business, the walls of this garage were covered in white laminate. The floor was painted deep-red and highly polished, there was a fifty inch TV on the wall that was hooked up to the internet for his traffic delays and roadworks, and it was also hooked up to his car for when Simon was out on the road. He looked back at his car as he opened the door at the back of his garage that took him into his office. His office furniture was very high end quality but this was just for him, nobody else seen it, nobody else ever came in, why would they, this was his den.

He had plenty of time on his hands, his pick up wasn't till the afternoon. So with that in mind, he had a look in the book. His pick up from airport was Mr Bay, he was one of Simon's many customers. He met him and his wife outside a club as he was driving past.

It was a rule of Simon's not to pick up on the street but they looked a nice couple and it turned out, Mr Bay's driver had let him down. That was two years ago and Simon has been his driver ever since. It was still too early to set off so he picked up the iPad from his desk and started to look down his emails, and even though there were a lot of emails that didn't interest him, nevertheless, he still looked through them, just to pass the time. But there was one email that jumped out at him, THE FAT CLUB. It looked like a sports supplement Warehouse, sign up now for free membership and up to fifty percent off on your first order. "That's not bad, worth a look later," he said to himself as he moved it to his save file. It was now time to make a move, he had three hours to get to where he needed to be. Even though the drive was only two hours' away, he always gave himself plenty of time just in case. He did his post checks before starting his car, Summer had already said when she went out for a drive with him that it was like being in a plane, but that's the way Simon did things. It's better to see a problem before it becomes a problem and he stuck by that. He arrived at the airport in good time and parked his car in the short stay car park, only because he had already checked the flight times and everything was running on time. He made his way through to arrivals and waited there in the crowd. It wasn't long before the first lot of passengers started to walk through. Simon held up his red square on a stick that he had got from the boot of this car. Mr Bay spotted it, and walked towards him.

"Good afternoon, sir," Simon said as he put the square down to his side.

"Good afternoon, Simon. How was the holiday?"

"Good, thank you, sir. Are you on your own today?"

Mr Bay passed him his case. "Yes, only me today. I left my business associate in Paris to finalise a deal." Mr Bay was in property, he started out ten years ago with a corner shop with a flat on top and now he has properties all over the world, he's known for being ruthless. Simon brought over his car and then stopped at the side of Mr Bay, he then got out, and walked around the car and opened the back door for him. Mr Bay then scanned the car whilst Simon put his case in the boot. This was a normal thing for Mr Bay, he always scanned the car before getting in as he made lots of calls which were very private.

"Take me to the Tufnell hotel please, Simon."

"Yes, sir," Simon put the address into his satnav even though he knew the hotel, he still put all journeys into his satnav, in case of roadworks or hold ups on the way. "We should be there in nineteen minutes, sir."

"Thank you, Simon." Simon then moved his rear view mirror down so he couldn't see Mr Bay as he was just about to take a call. It was one of Mr Bay's strict rules that Simon would not make eye contact with him whilst he was using his phone and it wasn't long before the air was blue with the hard language that Mr Bay would frequently use. Simon would often try and put his mind somewhere else but would always pick up on certain things that were said in his conversations. He had made the journey in good time to the Tufnell hotel, he slowly pulled up in the drop off lane. Mr Bay was still on his phone so Simon sat with his engine running.

"Okay, Simon, you can let me out now. I'll be two hours, if it's any different, I will call you, okay?" Simon got out and opened the door for him, and then waited until he had gone into the hotel.

After a short drive out of town, he pulled over on a small Industrial Estate, and sat and waited for his call, but also set his phone alarm to give him enough time to get back to the hotel just in case there was no call. He now had some free time to check his emails. THE FAT CLUB, this was the one that he was interested in and in just two clicks, he was on their website.

Welcome to the fat club, for all your fitness and sports supplement.

He had one hour to kill and that was plenty of time to fill in the membership form, it was the normal stuff which took ten minutes. He double clicked, and he was ready to buy protein, high calories in takes and fat burners for Summer. He was now done, how to pay options came up and he paid by PayPal with a next day delivery. It was now time to get going, the seven o'clock evening traffic was a little hectic but he still made it in good time. He waited at the main door of the hotel and when he could see Mr Bay, he got out of his car and opened the back passenger door. These were the little things that got Simon his work, it was all in the detail. Mr Bay walked down the steps to the car.

"Thank you, Simon," he said as Simon shut the door.

"Where to now, sir?"

"You can take me home, please, Simon," he said as he scanned the car. Simon once again pulled his rear view mirror down so he couldn't see as Mr Bay made another call.

The street lights reflected down on Simon's car, and the multicoloured lights from restaurants reflected back on the tinted windows as he drove through the town, and out on to the A roads and then eventually, turning on to a B road. He could see the lights coming up in the distance of Mr Bay's house, and every now and then, the lights would disappear as he drove around the bends. They eventually pulled up to the big brass gates of Mr Bay's house. Simon waited for Mr Bay to open the gates by using his app from his phone, as the gates slowly opened, he drove up to the house.

"Thank you, Simon. I'll need you in the morning between nine and ten. I'll text you the time is that okay?"

Simon looked back at him through his rear view mirror. "Yes, sir," he said as he eventually opened the car door for him. Simon then passed him his bag. "I'm going to book you for the rest of the week too." Simon closed the door and got back into his car setting off back down the driveway, and once again, the gates slowly opened, he pulled over to the side and waited for the gates to close behind him. He could hear the bolts locking into place one by one, he then pressed Mr Bay's intercom. "All locked, sir."

"Thank you, Simon." He then took off his tie rolled it up, and then set off back down the B road and within ten minutes, he was back on the A road and heading home.

As Simon drove down the road and on to the estate where he lived, he couldn't help but notice the televisions that were still on. It had just turned midnight and people were still up watching television. The different colours illuminated their living rooms giving each house, he looked, at a cosy feel. His own house was still in darkness only because Summer wasn't home. It was just a cold grey looking house but that's the way they were, even at Christmas they never put lights up, only because they were never there to enjoy them. The garage door opened as his car pulled on to his drive, the bright LED lights hurt his eyes as he drove in. His car was now parked up for the night, the bonnet of his car pinged with the heat of the engine. As he walked up his path to the house, a flood of lights came on, and the house came alive. No more was it cold and grey, it was now warm and inviting, but it was never the same when Summer wasn't home. The house always felt empty, it was just an empty space.

After two or three coffees, and quite a lot of cheese and biscuits, the stuff that nightmares were made of, it was now time for him to hit the sack. He heard Summer come in not long after. One hour later, he could feel her body pushing up against his, her hair was still wet from the shower she had just taken, but now he could relax knowing she was safely home, now he could get some sleep.

Chapter 2

Another day, another dollar.

That all familiar sound of the coffee maker gurgling in the background. Summer was up and in her dressing room. It was six in the morning and Simon had just brought her up a coffee.

"What time do you start work today?" Summer put her hair dryer down and had a taste of her coffee.

"That's nice. I'm on a twelve hour shift and I start at eight, so I'll be home for nine." Just then, he got a message from Mr Bay.

"Who is it?" Summer asked as she turned her hair dryer back on.

"It's from Mr Bay. He doesn't need me till midday, but he wants me to run him to Oxford for a meeting, and a second meeting first thing in the morning. So it looks like I won't be home tonight."

Summer said to him, "Make sure you take your overnight bag with you. You know what you're like, for forgetting things."

Simon smiled at her. "I know, I know," he said as he walked down the stairs. It was a pleasant morning, and Simon had been sat at his desk for just under an hour when he heard footsteps. He pushed back on his chair to see who it was.

"Okay then I'm off," Summer said. "Hopefully, I'll see you tomorrow. Drive carefully and ring me tonight when you book in at the hotel."

"Will do," he said and then blew her a kiss. Summer caught it in her hand as she walked to her car. She then waved at him as she drove away. Simon had some time to kill now, he poured himself a coffee from the pot he had in his office, then sat back in his chair and flicked through his work diary.

Things were definitely on the up, there just wasn't enough hours in the day. He now had to think about taking on another car and driver, and he had someone in mind for the job. The postman walked down Simon's drive, and as always, he was on time.

"Morning." Simon met him outside, he had some letters and a parcel for him. Simon placed the letters on his desk and then opened the parcel. It was from the fat club, and everything he had ordered was there with the invoice which was attached to a small piece of paper. It was an invitation to look around the company, he was the lucky winner of a draw and the slip of paper was his invite.

'You have been selected to attend a promotions day as one of our new customers.'

He noticed a phone number at the bottom of the paper. The fat club, Tables lane, Cumnor, with a postcode. Time was now getting on and he knew he had to do his car checks before setting off. He put the invite into his inside pocket as he did, his post checks on the car.

He eventually pulled up to Mr Bay's front gates, and before he push the intercom button, he sprayed the inside of the car with air freshener. The gates slowly opened as Simon drove through. He could see the camera's on the high poles following his car as he drove up to the house. He pulled to a slow stop at the front door where he waited until the door opened. There was Mr Bay. Simon got out of the car opening the back door as Mr Bay once again scanned the car.

"Morning, sir."

"Morning, Simon."

"Where to, sir?" Mr Bay gave him a postcode, the Royal Field Hotel, Oxford. The drive down to Oxford was long but a pleasant one, and as he pulled up to the hotel, one of the two hotel's doormen open Simon's back door.

Mr Bay said to Simon, "It's looking very likely my morning meeting will be at ten o'clock and I intend to be at least four hours, so I don't think I'll need you before three o'clock. Is it okay?"

"Yes, sir. Will you text me when you're ready, sir?"

"Yes, Simon, I will." And with that, Mr Bay got out of the car. The hotel doormen tried to take his bag but was welcomed with a staunch look. "No, that's okay. I can take it myself. Just take the case from the boot please." Simon waited until Mr Bay had walked into the main reception and then set off to his four star hotel which was only thirty minutes down the road. It was set in a small tree-lined driveway. The hotel he was staying for the night was quite nice, it had what you would say kerb appeal. He parked his car in the designated area, got his bag from the passenger side foot well. He learnt a long time ago that it was a mistake to put his bag in the boot, as it would always end up in some hotel by mistake. As he walked into the hotel, he couldn't help but notice the decor around him. It was as if he had just walked into the nineteen-forties. It was a lovely place, an elderly gentleman stood at the desk.

"Good afternoon, sir. Do you have a reservation? Could I take your name, sir?"

"Simon Rodgers.

"And your postcode, sir?" Simon passed on the information as well as his email address, and was then shown to his room.

"Breakfast is seven till nine. Would you like any papers in the morning?" Simon politely refused as he was given the key to his room. He was now on his own, his bag was on the bed and he had a look out of the window. He knew it wasn't the right time to ring Summer, so he pulled the slip of paper from his inside pocket, the fat club. He checked on Google maps for its location, it was only forty-two miles away from the hotel. He could get there in the morning and it would give him something to do with his free time. So with that in mind, he dropped the fat club an email, and within minutes, had received a message back.

'Nice to hear from you, Simon. We have booked you in for a tour of the factory. It starts at nine in the morning, please email us if you can attend.'

He emailed back, 'Yes, that's great. See you in the morning.'

He then received another email, 'Report to Miss Green on the front desk, please.'

He then sat in the chair, and once again, looked out of the window. It still wasn't time to ring Summer and there was nothing on the TV, even the coffee was instant. So he decided to take a shower to pass a bit of time. There was a light tap on his hotel door just as Simon was putting his shower robe on. "One minute, please." He opened the door to a young maid.

"Sir, dinner is about to finish. Would you like me to bring you some food to your room?"

"That would be fantastic."

She gave him the menu and politely said, "I will call back in ten minutes." He had no sooner looked at the menu when once again, there was a light tap on the door. The maid was back for the menu. He ordered spaghetti Bolognese and a glass of Montepulciano. This was as good as it could get, it was the sort of meal he would have at home with Summer. He now had enough time to give her a call before his meal arrived.

Summer was pleased to hear from him. Simon told her about his day as he always did when he was away from home. He told her all about the hotel, and how beautiful and quiet it was, and it was somewhere he would consider bringing her one day. He asked how her day had gone and so on. He had just put the phone down when the maid tapped on his door. The food smelt delicious as she wheeled it into his room.

"Enjoy, sir," she said as she pulled the door too. He rubbed his hands and tucked into his food, but still felt a little guilty that he wasn't home with Summer. But it soon passed when he had a taste of his Montepulciano, the meal was everything he knew it would be, and the wine went down a treat so much so, it made him sleepy, which was always a good thing, as he always found it hard to sleep when he was alone. But as his head touch the soft linen pillowcase, he was out like a light.

The birds singing outside the window woke Simon up before his alarm. It was six o'clock. He looked across to the chest of drawers with the instant coffee on top and thought better of it. Hopefully, they'll be ground coffee at the breakfast table, and he was right. He could smell the coffee as he walked down the winding staircase. He sat at the table in the corner near the window, out of the way of all the other guests. The first thing he ordered was a very large cup of coffee and then a full English breakfast. This wasn't heard of at home but when he was on business, a big breakfast would set him up for the day. He finished it with another large coffee. It was a lovely morning as he had packed his bag and put it in the foot well of his car, and was now doing his post drive checks and the fat club address was now in the satnav. It said he would be there in forty minutes. It wasn't long before he was driving through the town of Cumnor, such a lovely place. It was hard to believe there was an industrial estate on the outskirts of such a lovely little place like this, but as he turned the corner leading out of town, he could see the units on the left side of the road.

"You have reached your destination," his trusted satnav said as he turned on to the industrial estate. There were only five units and four of them were still under construction. Unit five was at the end.

It had a large sign that said, 'The fat club for all your dietary and sport's needs.' He pulled on to the car park with ten minutes to spare and then reset the satnav for the Royal Field Hotel, Oxford.

As Simon walked up to the unit, he noticed the red sign with white letters that said the fat club, and as he pulled open the large glass door to the reception, he noticed a lady sat at a desk, and again, a sign on the wall behind her that was the same as outside. "Good morning, sir. Can I help you?"

"Yes. My name is Mr Rodgers. I was told to be here for a walk round this morning."

"Please take a seat," the receptionist said as she picked up one of the three phones.

"Mr Rodgers is here to see you, sir. Yes, sir, I will." She put the phone down. "He will be with you shortly, sir." Simon sat back and looked around the room. Awards were placed on the walls for business achievements, two large yucca plants were placed at the door to the factory floor. He noticed a nameplate on the receptionist desk which said Jessica Green. Everything on her desk was in its place.

Just then, one of the phones rang. "Good morning, the fat club, Jessica speaking. And your order number is? Yes, okay. I'll see what I can do."

And then, another phone rang. "Good morning. FAT, yes, sir. I'll get him to give you a call." Jessica put the phone down and looked at Simon and smiled. Simon smiled back at her but not knowing what he was smiling about. Just as the door to the factory floor opened, in walked a small man and slightly overweight. Simon put him at about seventy-five years old. Jessica got up from her desk. "Sir, may I introduce Mr Simon Rodgers?"

"Thank you, Jessica." The man held out his hand to Simon. "Good morning. May I call you Simon?"

Simon got up from his chair feeling slightly nervous, why he didn't know. "Yes, sir."

"Good. I'm pleased to meet you, Simon. You may call me Teddy. Did you have a pleasant journey here?"

"Yes, sir," Simon said. "I stayed at a nice little hotel last night as I dropped one of my clients off in Oxford."

"Right, and what hotel did you stay in?"

"It's called the blue chalk hotel."

"Ah, yes. I have heard of it, and how was your stay?" Simon was feeling more relaxed now, he hadn't realised what Teddy had just done. "Shall we go in and I'll show you what we do here."

Simon said, "You supply supplements to the public, don't you?"

"Yes, of course, we do. Come with me, I'll show you around." Teddy put his white pass card against a fob on the wall which opened an airtight door. The bright lights hit Simon's eyes as he walked through the door which closed behind them.

"So, Simon, this is where we store all our products and as you can see everything is in its place." He noticed there were four walkways, and the racking was two pallets high and the floor was so clean you could have eaten your dinner off it. It just didn't look right. Teddy stopped at the canteen, there were seven people sat in white overalls, it was all so very clean, it just didn't look right.

The next hour was all about the fat club as a business and how it was started up, and where they are at present day.

"So, Simon, are you happy with what you have seen? If so I'll take you up to my office for some refreshments, please follow me." Teddy walk down to the opposite side of the unit to where the offices where to a door. He then put his thumb on to a small square plate on the wall and another door slid open. "This way, Simon," he said as he put his hand on Simon's back to reassure him. And within seconds, Simon was in Teddy's office. "Why do you think you're here today?"

Simon looked around the room and then back at Teddy. "Because I won a competition for a walk round your company."

Teddy looked straight into his eyes. "NO," he said. "That's not why you're here." Simon was now very nervous, his palms were sweaty. He had a habit of tapping his knees when he was nervous. The lift door opened, Simon turned to see who it was. "Come in, Joseph."

"Good morning, Teddy. Here is the folder." He placed it down on the right hand side of Teddy's desk and then sat at the back of the office behind Simon. Teddy pulled the large paper clip that was holding the file together and then looked at Simon.

"You went to Carnhill High School and left school with no grades." Simon looked at him. "And looking at your files, you were not the brightest in school. You worked in a supermarket but then you were sacked for bad time keeping." Simon again looked at him in disbelief as Teddy turned to the next page. "You then, as a young boy, got a job with a small transport haulier and stayed with them for six years. You then had some time off moving around, and finally started working for a company and stayed with them for twenty-two years and took early redundancy. You then started your own company with the help of the bank."

Simon got to his feet. "I think I should go now."

Joseph got up at the same time to cover the exit. "SIT DOWN, SIMON," he said as he undone the button on his jacket. Simon had no choice but to do as he said.

Teddy turned another page of his file. "Nobody is going to hurt you, Simon. So can I carry on? You got married to Summer in 2003, July the sixth."

Simon got to his feet once again. "I've had enough of this now. What is going on, what do you want with me, what have I done?"

Teddy closed the file and put his hands on top of it. Simon sat back down but was now very nervous. Teddy called Joseph over and he sat next to Simon, nothing was said for a minute or two, they just looked at him. The phone rang and Teddy answered it quite abruptly. "Not now," he said and put the phone back down.

"Right, Simon, we've had you under surveillance for eight months." Simon could not believe what he was hearing, why was this happening to him.

Joseph put his hand on his shoulder to reassure him. "You're here, hopefully, to help us, do you understand what we have just said?"

Simon looked at Joseph and then Teddy. "No, I don't. You're a company that sells sports supplements, aren't you?"

"Yes and no," Joseph said. "I think it's time to explain, Teddy. Don't you?" Teddy sat upright on his chair.

Chapter 3

"Tell me about Mr Bay. You know him, you drive for him, you've drove for him for the last two years, but how well do you know him," Teddy was straight to the point no holding back. Simon's mouth was now drying up. "Are you okay, Simon? Would you like a cup of tea? Joseph, could you ring down for a pot of tea. I think we could all do with some, don't you?"

"Now where was I? How well do you know him?"

Simon shuffled in his seat. "Yes, I've known him for some time."

"Tell me about him."

"Well, he's a very reserved person who keeps himself to himself. I'm not going to say anymore till you tell me what's going on."

Just then, the tea arrived. Joseph waited as the lift door opened, and there was the tea trolley. Joseph pushed it into the room. "Tea for three," Joseph said. "And one will be mine."

Teddy took a sip of his tea. "Lovely cup, Joseph."

"Thank you, sir. You asked who we are, Simon. Well, I will tell you, we are the fat club."

"Right," Simon said. "You're the fat club."

Joseph put his cup on the trolley. "We run an organisation that is government funded, it's called the fat club which stands for 'Fight Against Terrorism'."

Teddy thanked Joseph for explaining. "So you see, Simon, you are now in the recruitment centre, and like I said before, we've had our eye on you for some time now and we needed to get you in to have a little word. We would like you to help us get our man. So let's tell you a bit about your ever so polite Mr Bay."

"He started out as a young boy who came into the UK with his parents and eventually, they opened a corner shop. Mr Bay's first name is Lawrence, he grew up on the streets and mixed with the wrong people. After his parents both passed away, the shop was left to him and that's where his empire began. It was in the early days when Mr Bay made his mark, he raised a loan on his property, and got into money lending and the riff-raff he knocked about with as a young boy became the hard men. The business became very lucrative so he bought into property to let, in the UK and in Europe as holiday homes. He then got into second hand car dealerships in the UK and Ireland. We also know that he deals in illegal contraband and some gun-running, and uses his letting business as a cover to get around, but the worrying thing is, we think he may now be bringing in contract killers as another business line. We need to put a stop to him once and for all, and that's where you come in, Simon."

"No, no, no," Simon said as he walked around the room. "Are you mad? I'm a driver. Are you mad? I could die."

Joseph once again calmed him down. "Simon, everything will be okay, nothing can go wrong. We will be with you every step of the way, trust us."

Simon sat back down, his head in his hands, saying no over and over again.

It was now Teddy's turn to stand. "Okay, Simon. I understand how you feel and you're free to go. But before you do, let me say this, we know Mr Bay is getting contract killers into the country but we don't know how. But let me say this to you, what if one of them shot your wife as she was leaving the hospital by mistake. How would you feel then? So where are your morals? It could be somebody's wife, husband or even somebody's child, could you live with that if you read it in the newspapers the following week?"

Simon got up and walked towards the lift doors saying, "This is not my problem."

Joseph said to him, “But it is now because you know about it, don’t you?”

The lift door opened and Simon turned to Teddy, “If I go along with this, what would I have to do?”

Joseph pulled his hand away from the door. “Come and sit down, and tell us everything you know about him. We have to find a way into his world in order for this to work.” Now they knew Simon was on board, things were definitely different.

Teddy opened a small notebook from his inside pocket. “Right. How does Mr Bay contact you?”

“By text, and sometimes he’ll book one month in front, depending on his work load. But then I get a month’s payment if I’m used or not.”

“Do you ever get to see anything that goes on?”

Simon looked at Joseph, “What does he mean?”

Joseph explained, “You know, do you ever see Mr Bay with anybody else? Does anybody ever give him any packages or envelopes?”

“No, he’s a very reserved person. If I take him to a hotel, I wait in the car till I see him actually go into the hotel and that’s the same with the airport.”

Teddy tapped his pen on his notebook. “What about when you pick him up from the hotel?

“He’ll text me with a pick up time and I wait outside. I never go in. At the airport, I wait in the pickup area but he’s always on his own.”

“Do you ever get to hear any of his telephone conversation?”

“No, not really.”

Teddy looked at Joseph. “We’re fighting a losing battle here. Is there anything at all even though you think it may be a bit silly?”

Simon sat back into his chair. “There is one thing he always does.”

“And what’s that?”

“Well, before he gets into the car, he scans it.”

"What did you say?" Teddy looked at Joseph. "What did you say, Simon?"

"Before Mr Bay gets in my car, he scans it."

"With what?"

"With a scanner."

"Yes, I get that, but how does he scan it?"

Simon looked at them both. "With his phone, of course."

"That's it, Joseph. That's why we've never been able to get him because he has an electronic listening device scanner fitted into his phone. Our Mr Bay is a cool customer, but now we're getting somewhere. So, Simon, tell us again what you do when you pick Mr Bay up?"

Simon went through everything again, "I get a text from him for a pick up time. I normally get there ten minutes early, and sit and wait. I then open the back door as you do, and then wait as he scans the car. Once I get the all clear, I shut the door behind him, and then settle down into my seat and set off to the postcode he has given me. If at any time he makes a phone call, I pull my rear view mirror down."

"STOP," Joseph said as he looked at Teddy. "Why do you do that, Simon?"

"Because Mr Bay doesn't like to be seen whilst he's on the phone."

"So, Simon, when he has finished his phone call, do you put your mirror back up."

"Yes, of course, I do."

"That's it, Joseph, we have him."

Joseph turned to Simon patting him on the back and smiled. Now then, were getting somewhere, Teddy asked if he was okay for time. Simon looked down at his watch. "Yes, I'm okay."

"Good. So then this is what we're going to do."

Teddy asked Joseph to carry on. "Right, Simon, we're going to fit a device into your car. It will be fitted into your car speakers, and will automatically connect to his phone signal and pick up any calls Mr Bay receives and record them."

"But how is that going to work when you both know that Mr Bay scans the car before he gets into it?"

"Yes, but that's where you come in. What we want you to do is just push the button, that's all. You said you have to put your mirror down, that's right, isn't it? Explain to Simon how were going to do it, Joseph."

"We're going to fit a small switch on the back of your mirror and this is how it's going to work. When you pick Mr Bay up, he scans the car before he gets in, right?" Simon nodded his head. "So once he's in the car, the scanner has done its job, right?" Simon nodded his head again.

"Right then, when Mr Bay makes a call and you pull the mirror down, you will then press the switch. That will then activate the device that will automatically connect to his phone and the job is done." Simon didn't nod his head. It wasn't the reaction Teddy and Joseph were expecting.

"How do we know it will work?"

Joseph reassured him, "Trust me, Simon, it will work. You have absolutely nothing to worry about."

Teddy finished his now cup of cold tea. "Now all we need to do is get this fitted to Simon's car without it being suspicious and anybody knowing. Let's be honest, we don't know if Mr Bay has eyes on Simon, do we?"

Simon cut in on the conversation, "Wait a minute, if he's got eyes on me as you say, then he'll know I'm here with you now."

"No, Simon," Joseph said. "You're at the fat club on a promotions day, with free gifts that you will conveniently leave on your front seat just so Mr Bay will see, and he will ask you about it, trust me. But what we need to do now is somehow get your car into a garage so we can get the device fitted."

"Well, that's easy to do," Simon said. "My car's due a major service very soon."

Teddy rubbed his hands together. "See it's all coming together now, isn't it? You just leave that part to us, we have your mobile number if we need to get hold of you, and if you need to get hold of me or Joseph, you must ring the fat club and ask for orders. They will ask you for a promotion code. Simon, this is your code number, don't forget it, it's j.t.h.y.h.1.9.5.6.1.9.6.3, have you got that? This code number will go straight to me or Joseph we will then take your call and tell you what to do."

Teddy looked at the monitor on his desk. "Ah, just in time. It's Jessica with the paper work."

The lift doors opened and in she walked. "Here you are, sir. As requested." She placed them down on his desk in front of him.

"Right, Simon. Let's get down to business, have a read of this, and if you will please, sign it at the bottom."

Simon pulled his chair up to the desk. "Hang on a minute. What's this? Why do I have to sign this?

Joseph explained to him, "This is the official secrets act. You have to sigh it or we cannot continue. Once you have signed it, you cannot talk to anyone, not even your wife, do you understand? And don't worry, you're not signing up to be a secret agent. You can leave that to us." Teddy pushed the pen in front of him and Simon signed it but couldn't help but wonder what the hell he had got himself into. Teddy picked up the document, and made sure he had signed and dated it, and then passed it on to Jessica.

"Thank you, sir. And, Mr Rodgers, your goodie bag will be in reception." The lift door opened once more and off she walked. She was like a model on the catwalk.

"Right then, I think we're done here. Have you anything to say? Joseph looked at him.

"I think we've covered everything, don't you, Simon?" He nodded. Teddy then stood up from his desk. "Right, Simon, I'll walk you out." All three of them walked to the lift. "Well, Simon, Joseph will take you to reception and let you get on your way. We don't want you to be late for Mr Bay, do we?"

Simon walked away from the unit with his goodie bag placing it on the front passenger seat of his car. His world was now a different place, his carefree attitude have somewhat disappeared into space, and now his mind was on Mr Bay. Not about getting there on time but trying not to look suspicious, and how he hated the fact that he ever picked him up that evening in the first place. But then he thought of Summer and what she always said to him, things happen for a reason and that's karma, the phrase she always uses is what goes around comes around. He started his car and pulled up to the exit of the car park looking back at the building. Nothing looked out of place, Jessica was sat at her desk, she didn't look up; she didn't acknowledge him. He felt like he had been there all day, he still had plenty of time on his hands before he had to pick up Mr Bay, and he had plenty of time to go over in his mind, as he made his way back to the hotel. The journey back was short but tedious, his heads up display showed an incoming text message from Mr Bay. It said, 'Morning, Simon. Meeting nearly at an end, you may pick me up at two thirty.'

Simon said on his voice commands, "Received with thanks." His heads up display showed a message sent. Just for a minute, Simon had palpitations but they soon past. *I can't go through with his, I'm a nervous wreck.* He wanted nothing more than to just drive past the hotel and just keep on going. But now he knew all about Mr Bay, and that made him very nervous.

'You have arrived at your destination.' He turned off his satnav as he turned into the hotel car park with minutes to spare. His palms were sweating as he sat and waited. Eventually, Mr Bay walked out on to the steps of the main entrance of the hotel. Simon drove up to meet him once again. Mr Bay scanned the car before getting in. Simon was looking at things differently now.

"Good afternoon, sir. Did everything go as well as planned?"

"Yes, it did, Simon. Thank you for asking." Mr Bay then looked over to the front seat. "Have you been shopping?"

Simon smiled. "Yes, sir, I have. Where would you like to go now, sir?"

Mr Bay sat back into his seat. "I would like to go home but I will need you to do a slight detour to a property I'm thinking of purchasing." Mr Bay gave Simon the postcode and started to go through his paperwork from the meeting. It was a pleasant afternoon as Simon drove through the city and out on to the outskirts. He had been driving for about twenty minutes or so when Mr Bay asked him to pull over and slow down. Simon looked at his satnav. He still had a good ten minutes to go before he was at the postcode.

"Are you sure, sir? This isn't the postcode I put in the satnav."

"Yes, I know but this property has also got my attention." The property he was looking at was of a modest size and quite secluded.

"Would you like me to stop, sir? Maybe you would like to look around?"

"No, Simon, just pull over." Mr Bay dropped his window down a little. He glanced at the property and the surrounding area, he liked what he had seen.

"Simon, what's the house number?"

"Nineteen, sir."

Mr Bay got the house details up on line. "Not bad for the money, not bad at all." He then dialled a number on his phone, and as he did so, he looked up at Simon. Simon sat back and pulled his rear view mirror down so not to see him. It only took five minutes or so and it was all done. Simon had guessed what had happened.

"Okay, Simon, you can continue." He started his car. Mr Bay told him, "You don't have to go to the next property, you can take me home please." Simon had guessed right, the deal was done. Mr Bay put his window up and sat back into his seat for the journey home.

The day was nearly at an end as Simon drove up on to his drive. His garage door opened as he pulled forward. It had been a long day and he was worn out, there was a lot going round in this head which had now given him a headache. The garage door closed behind him, and he decided to do his posts ops checks in the morning. That was not like him at all, he was mentally exhausted.

The house was in a quiet state. Summer was tucked up in bed, and although he just wanted to go to sleep, he decided to have a coffee instead. Now the panic set in, he sat at the island in his kitchen. His hands were sweating again, he couldn't hold his coffee mug because of his hands trembling. Anxiety had set in and then he noticed he was sat in the dark. He thought, what right did these people have to get him involved in this, what right did Teddy and Joseph have.

"Are you okay, Simon? Why are you sat in the dark?" He turned round his nerves were on edge. It was Summer. "What's up, Simon?"

"I have a very bad headache." Summer put her warm hand on his forehead and just for a moment, Simon wanted to tell her all about it, just to share the burden but he knew he couldn't because of what he had signed. But most of all, he couldn't do something like that to his beloved Summer. It was going to be a long night ahead. Even though Mr Bay had told him he wasn't needed for tomorrow, it didn't really help him in anyway. He tossed and turned for most of the night, plus every now and then, his phone would light up on his bedside drawers to indicate he had a new email. The night eventually passed and after a bad night, Simon woke up at ten in the morning. Summer had let him sleep in, which wasn't at all like her. His headache had almost gone now, he just lay there listening to the birds singing outside. Yesterday was one of those days he would never forget, not in a long time but he was in a better frame of mind now. Teddy and Joseph did say to him that Mr Bay will never know, and Joseph did say no body will hurt you. Simon threw back the covers off the bed, feet on the floor.

"It's another day," he said to himself as he walked into the en suite for his shower. He had the full day to himself as Mr Bay had made other plans for the day so Simon wasn't needed. He felt better after his hot shower and sat in his front room having his first morning coffee when his iPad lit up. Email from the fat club, Simon opened to the page.

'Hi, Simon. We have some new promotional offers, please ring the number below and have your promotional code ready.' Simon looked out of his window, he felt like everything was closing in on him again. He picked his iPad up and put the phone number into his phone to ring later. After having his breakfast and his workout in the gym, Simon finally sat down at his office desk. He took a deep breath and rang the number on his phone.

"Good morning, the fat club. Can I help you, sir?"

"Yes, good morning. This is Mr Rodgers. I've had an email from your company with regards to a promotional offer."

"Okay, sir. Can I take your promotional code?"

Simon said very clearly, "j.t.h.y.h.1.9.5.6.1.9.6.3."

The line went silent. He waited. "Putting you through now, sir."

"FAT, can I help?" Simon instantly recognised the voice, it was Jessica Green.

"I've had an email to ring in."

"Morning, Simon. Are you well?"

"Yes, as well as can be."

"Well, that's good to hear. I have some information for you. As you know your car will be in for a service soon, we would like you to let the reception know that you're having your air conditioning serviced by an independent company called Straight Line Air Conditioning. We have now set that company up and will be expected a call from your garage very soon. Once your car has been fitted with the listening device, you will be contacted again. So all you have to do is just drop off the car and pick it up as normal. Okay, Simon, anything you're not sure about?"

Simon once again went silent in disbelief, he could only say okay. Jessica said, "Don't forget your service date, and it's very important that you keep it. Thank you, good day, sir." The line went dead, Simon put his phone on the desk and just sat there looking at it. What had he got himself into and not only that, how was he going to get himself out of it. As the day passed on, the more anxious he got. Even the slightest noise made him jittery. So to say he was nervous was an understatement and the fact that he hadn't actually done anything yet, and he still had a long way to go. Well, what could he do but only resign himself to the fact that whatever happens, happens, and as he sat there alone, even at his age he reminded himself that nothing is free in this world and if it sounds too good to be true, then it isn't. The weeks past and everything ran the same as it always did. Everyone was happy with Simon's service including Mr Bay, and that morning, Simon got his letter from the car company stating his service date which was due in the next couple of days.

Chapter 4

Simon hadn't heard from the fat club but then again, Jessica did say that he wouldn't. The rest of the day belonged to him. He was going to have a cold beer in the garden and just watch the day roll by. He also had an easy day tomorrow as he was going to be driving a wealthy businessman's wife around the shops. A nice easy day and then the day after his car was going in for service. The following morning, Simon woke up to Summer's shuffling.

"What time is it?" he said as he fumbled with the light on his watch.

"It's four thirty, go back to sleep." But to Simon that was like saying do you want a free supply of coffee for the year. Once he was awake, there was no going back to sleep. The first thing he needed was his coffee fix. Summer eventually came into the kitchen for a chat. They talked about everything and anything as she kept one eye on the time. She placed her cup on the worktop and turned to him.

"What time will you be home?

Simon put her cup into the dishwasher. "It shouldn't be late. I'll more than likely be home before you." Summer then took the car keys from her bag. "And think on, don't mess with the television because I have things recording that I would like to watch when you're not here."

Simon raised his eyebrow. "For one minute, I thought you were going to miss me."

Summer looked back at him as she walked through the kitchen and out into the hall. "Yes that too," she said.

It was a gorgeous day as Simon pulled on to the forecourt of the main dealers. His phone rang, it was Jessica Green; he answered it with caution.

"Are you at the garage, Mr Rodgers? Our people are waiting to come in."

"Yes, I've just got here."

"Thank you, Mr Rodgers," she said and then just hung up. Simon thought what an unpleasant lady she actually is. His car was now parked in one of the service pads, he did his walk round before booking it in, taking pictures of each side, and front and back of the car with his phone just so he could check it later.

"Good morning, sir. How may I help you?"

Simon put his service book on to the counter. "My name's Mr Rodgers. I'm booked in for a service."

"Ah, yes, sir. You're booked in on a fast track. Is that right, sir?" Simon nodded his head and also said he has an independent company called Straight Line Air Conditioning coming into service the car's air conditioning. The receptionist looked up his particulars. "Yes that's right, Mr Rodgers. We have booked you in for lunch at the Hare and Hounds it's just around the corner."

As Simon walked out on to the forecourt, he noticed a black van with silver writing on the side. It said, 'STRAIGHT LINE'. He didn't know the driver but he recognised the lady in the passenger seat from the canteen when he first met Teddy and Joseph. He looked back at the van as it drove past him and noticed the lady was looking in her side mirror at him.

Steak and ale pie was on the menu at the Hare and Hounds, and it wasn't long before he was tucking into it with a hot mug of tea and then apple pie and custard to follow. Two hours had passed when he got a text, it was from the fat club. 'Your order is now ready for collection.' This could only mean his car was now fitted with the listening device. At the end of the text, it said, 'please use your promotional code to see what other products are available.'

It wasn't long after he got his call from the garage to collect his car. Simon checked around the car, and they gave him his service documentation and a receipt from STRAIGHT LINE. The rest of the day was his, and as he drove back home, he couldn't stop looking at his rear view mirror. There was nothing different that he could see, no button. What crossed his mind was, could they not fit the device, had there been a problem, could this be the end of the matter, could he get on with his life again.

He had got home in good time. His car was running like a dream but then it always did. First things first, Simon made himself a coffee sat down and then rang the fat club.

"Fat club. Good afternoon, can I take your promotional code?" Simon give them his code. "Thank you, sir, transferring you now."

Jessica Green was now on the line. "Mr Rodgers, we've been waiting for your call, putting you through now."

"Ah, Simon, how did it go? We've been told the device is now fully fitted to your car." It was the unmistakable voice of Teddy.

Simon felt as if his stomach had just been ripped out. There was a short silence. "Are you there, Simon? It's Teddy here."

Simon put his coffee on the small table next to him. "Yes, I'm here."

"Ah, good. We need you to meet someone who can go over the device and bring you up to speed. It has to be sooner than later."

Simon said, "Tuesday, if that's okay."

Again, there was silence. "Yes that's okay, Simon. We can do that. Our man will call you, you will be driving him to Heathrow airport. He's heading out to Brussels on business so that will be perfect, thank you."

The line went dead, and then Jessica answered, "Okay, Mr Rodgers, so we're quite clear what we are doing."

"Yes," Simon said. But that's all he could say.

"Then I bid you good day, Mr Rodgers." It was the time of day when Summer would be arriving home from work and how he needed to see her now. He needed her close to him, he needed to tell someone so he could off load the problem. The worry was unbearable, he just couldn't tolerate it anymore. But then he knew if he said anything then the cat was let out of the bag, he would definitely go to prison for treason. At last, he could see Summer's car as she drove up to the drive and could smell her perfume as she walked into the house.

"How did it go with the car service today? Only you look a bit worried."

"No, it went well, no problems."

"Good," Summer said as she walked up the stairs for a shower. That evening, they talked for most of the night.

The next day was business as usual. Simon was out running clients around when a text came through on his car system. It was the fat club, they wanted to know when he was free to talk. He voice texted them back, "Free in ten minutes." He then found a safe place to park after dropping his client off and then rang the fat club. Giving them his code number he was then put through to a Mr Robyn. He was a softly spoken man, and seemed very polite, not at all what he was expecting. He asked if he could be collected at nine in the morning on Tuesday as he had an afternoon flight but needed some time with Simon. They made their arrangements, and Mr Robyn said how nice it was to speak to him and then he put the phone down.

For the first time, Simon felt a little more relaxed after the conversation with him. It was just enough time before he got the call to pick up the footballers wag he was driving for.

The rest of the week passed without any hick ups and Tuesday was soon upon him.

He had his coffee that morning, and did all the post drive checks and had the postcode for his pick up, and had plenty of time to get there. His mind wandered just a little on the way down the motorway but his mind was still on his driving. Although he couldn't help but think what Mr Robyn looked like, he was trying to put the face to the soft voice.

The satnav took him to a Victorian three-storey house in a nice area of the town. He stopped and waited outside, and shortly after, the front door opened to reveal Mr Robyn, a somewhat short man about five foot two or maybe four, very slim in build and was very smartly dressed. Simon met him on the stairs to take his overnight bag.

"Morning, Simon. My name's Sinclair Robyn. It's a lovely morning, isn't it?" Simon nodded his head. He had instantly took a liking to him.

He put Mr Robyn's bag in the boot and then made sure he was comfortable before setting off. Once they were on their way, Mr Robyn started the conversation by saying,

"So, good morning, Simon. As you know my name is Mr Robyn but please call me Sinclair. I am here to give you a heads up on where we are at the moment. Teddy and Joseph have told me you're fully on board, and I trust their judgement. As you know your car has been fitted with the listening device," Simon looked at him in his rear view mirror and nodded. "Right, if you hold your rear view mirror and move it down, you'll feel a small raised button. That will turn the device on.

There will be a small red light that will illuminate but don't worry, anyone in the car will think it's the rear view anti dazzle position. But don't forget to turn it off when you put the mirror up. It's very important that you do this, Simon." Again, Simon nodded. Mr Robyn then opened his case, and took some paperwork out and placed it on his lap. "I now have some information for you about your man Mr Bay. He's going to smuggle this person into the country. I can honestly say we have been worried about this person for some time. They call him Westesson Kite, he originates from Switzerland. Our man overseas has had him covered for some time now and has now reported to us that he's now on the move. I have a picture of him and will show you when we get to the airport."

Simon interrupted him, "Hang on a minute, sir. Why do I need to see a picture of this man when I'm only supposed to be recording Mr Bay?"

"Please, Simon, call me Sinclair. The reason why I'm showing you this picture is because he's a very dangerous man and in the event that you meet him, you must abort the operation no matter what. Your safety is imperative, we have never asked a civilian to go on an undercover operation like this before, but we have no choice. You have built up a trust with Mr Bay and Kite is a very dangerous man, so you must know your limits.

You will do well, Simon, from what Teddy and Joseph have said about you, and what I had seen today, I know you are the right man for the job."

Simon felt quite proud of what Mr Robyn had just said but he was still having palpitations, not that there was anything wrong he just got so worked up.

They talked about each other the rest of the way to the airport. Simon had told him his life story, where Mr Robyn only told him what he needed him to know. It was time for them to part company. Mr Robyn showed him the picture of the Kite. He was your typical stereo type from

Switzerland, blonde hair, blue eyes and well built but quite a cold-looking person. He now understood what Mr Robyn was saying. Simon got his bag from the boot and shook his hand. Mr Robyn told him to be very careful and looked forward to maybe meeting him again, and with that, he turned and disappeared into the crowd. Simon was left standing at his car.

The drive home was busy. He could smell Mr Robyn's aftershave. It was a very unusual smell but nice. He would definitely recognise it again, he set the car on cruise control and put his classical music on, and made his way through the heavy traffic on the motorway and once again, he had time to reflect about the mess he had got himself into. He had put it on par with someone on death row, he knew the date was coming but didn't know when.

He just wanted it over and done with now. He just wanted his life back, just to be normal again. He was now driving down familiar roads in his hometown, he was nearly home.

Summer was home when he pulled up on to the drive. She had got away early and welcomed him with a lovely smell of what she was preparing for the evening meal.

"Now that smells really good, it should do."

"It's your favourite; it's Italian meatballs and there's a glass of wine on the side for you, and you have an email. It's from that company called the fat club."

Simon nearly dropped his wine glass. "Have I got time to have a look at it?"

"Of course, you have. I'll be plating it out in ten minutes." He put his promotional code into the site.

'Order confirmation. Your order has been sent. IT'S NOW ON, YOU WILL BE CONTACTED TOMORROW.'

That evening was so lovely. The doors to the back garden were wide open, a light breeze blew through into the kitchen diner. Simon knew as from tomorrow, the game was on. Summer was on an early shift that morning, and was up and out of the door by five am. She left Simon in bed to sleep. His first pick up wasn't till one in the afternoon so the morning was his.

He finally got up around ten and got ready but before setting off, he jumped on to the fat club site. The response back was fast, it was as if they were waiting for him. 'Ring Jessica Green #.' He looked across at the clock on the kitchen wall, he had enough time to call her before setting off.

"Good morning, fat club. It's Simon Rodgers here."

"Ah, Simon. Do you have your promotional code?" He promptly gave it to her.

"Hold the line, Simon." And within seconds, he was put through to Teddy.

"Morning, Simon. Hope you're well. I won't beat around the bush. Our man overseas has now confirmed that the Kite is definitely on the move. So it's definitely on now, Simon. So every time you drive for Mr Bay, you must have the listening device on, and, Simon, be very careful. We will be able to listen in, on conversations and track your location."

Simon asked if he could ask a question before Teddy hung up. "Yes, Simon, fire away."

He asked the question, "How will I know if you have the information you need?"

Teddy answered, "You will get emails every evening with an update. Anything else before I go?"

Simon said, “No.” But knew as soon as he put the phone down, he would think of something that he should have asked.

The next morning, Simon was up and ready to go. He had gone over his car with a fine toothcomb. Nothing was out of place, but then everything was always in place, but he was on edge so he double-checked everything.

He switched the listening device on and off that many times, it was as if he had Obsessive Compulsive Disorder and had to stop just in case he did any damage to it.

The drive over to Mr Bay’s house was as it had always been, nice and pleasant. The large gates opened slowly on his arrival and as he drove up to the front doors, Mr Bay opened them with his wife at his side. She kissed him on the cheek and then waved at Simon. Simon waved back at her whilst saying under his breath, “Please work, please work. Mr Bay walked to the car with his phone in his hand but then stopped and looked at Simon then looked down at his phone again, Simon held his breath just for a moment. It was all too much for Simon, in all the panic, he had forgotten to open the car door for Mr Bay. He resumed his composure and opened the door. “Sorry, sir.

“Are you okay, Simon? This isn’t like you. Is everything okay at home?”

“Yes, sir. I had a sleepless night but I’m perfectly okay to drive you today,” he said this to put Mr Bay’s mind at rest. The day ahead was going to be a long one. Mr Bay had four people to see and had given Simon the postcodes, and he had put them into the satnav in the order they had been given, but the day was going to be long for other reasons that only Simon knew about. They were five minutes into the journey when Mr Bay’s phone rang. Simon pulled his mirror down and touched the button at the same time. This was it but as Simon picked up certain words from Mr Bay’s conversation, he soon realised it was his wife. It then became obvious that Mr Bay had left something at home. When he had finished his call, Simon pulled the mirror back up and touched the button once more. That was the only phone call that day, even though Mr Bay had four appointments. Simon came to the conclusion that all his business details must have been done behind closed doors. Later on that evening, Simon had a call from Joseph after going through the correct channels. Joseph told him it was Mr Bay's wife that had rang him. It was as Simon had expected, but then it was a good thing because it had given them time to check the listening device and to make sure it was working okay. But to Simon it felt like a nail had been pushed into his coffin.

When will this end, he said to himself. He thought this was going to be a quick fix, but it was now beginning to be a long, drawn-out problem. Even Summer could see a change in him, he was becoming very jittery, and was always nervous and unable to relax.

His job was now becoming a heavy burden, his marriage wasn't on the rocks but Summer would often work late just to save having any arguments. This was only because he was under so much stress, not a day went by when Simon wished he had never got involved with the whole thing.

Another day was coming to an end and there he was, in bed by himself. The front door opened and then softly closed. He picked up his phone that was on the floor next to him, it was one o'clock in the morning and another hour passed before Summer came into the bedroom. Simon could see she had been crying as she sat on the end of the bed. She asked Simon out right, "Who is she?"

Simon sat upright putting the bedside light on. He couldn't believe what Summer had just said, but now the whole thing was getting out of hand. He stopped and thought for a moment, what if the shoe was of the other foot, how would he be feeling, and yes Summer was right in what she had just said to him. Simon looked at her. "I have to tell you something." Summer's eyes welled up once more, her head was down and she looked as if her world had just come to an end. He took her hand and held it tight. "It's nothing like that," he said. "But I have to get something off my chest." She looked at him with open eyes. "It all started when we got back from holiday. As you know, I'm always looking around for deals on the internet, and that's when I came across the fat club. They emailed me with some of their offers, but now I know it was too good to be true."

Summer asked him, "Why?"

"Well, I then placed an order with them and then they said I had been picked out of the hat so to speak, and I was invited to go down to their warehouse to have a look around and also get some free promotional items. When I got there, they knew who I was."

Summer looked at him. "Well, they will know who you are because they've just invited you. Where is this going, Simon?"

He took a hold of her hand once more. "Summer, you asked me what I was getting up to so please let me finish. When I got there, they knew my name, they knew your name, they knew what your job was, they knew everything about us."

Summer pulled her hand away from his. "What have you got yourself into, Simon?"

He put his head down. "I'm in a right mess, Summer, a right mess. I'm not having an affair, can you see that now?"

Summer got up and walked towards the window. "So what have they got you doing for them. Tell me it's not drugs."

Simon sat up on the end of the bed. "No, it isn't anything like that. I had to sign a document for the official secrets act, it's something to do with national security."

Summer turned to him. "Are you having a laugh, do you really expect me to believe all this rubbish?"

"It's the truth, trust me." And for the next hour or so, Simon sat down with Summer and told her everything. He left nothing, not a single thing out, his cards were out on the table.

Dawn was breaking and everything had been said that needed to be said, and Simon felt better for it. But now he knew he had put some of the burden on to Summer's shoulders, and it was a particularly heavy burden. Summer told him that she was going to have it out with this Teddy person. "I'm going to give him a piece of my mind."

Once again, Simon had to say, "You can't, Summer. I'll go to jail. I just have to go through with this. But now I know I have you on my side, it now makes it more possible to get away with it."

They hadn't really slept that night. Summer rang her work to say she had a bad night and was going to take a day's holiday. But for Simon, his book was full for the day but his first pick up wasn't till nine o'clock, and it didn't involve Mr Bay. He looked out of the window. Once again, it was so peaceful at that time in the morning. He felt Summer's hands go around his waist and a soft kiss on his neck, that was just what he needed. Everything was now going to be alright, that was as long as he could get through the mess he had gotten himself into. She gave him one last hug and placed her chin on his shoulder saying everything would be alright. That was enough for him, he just broke down in a flood of tears, tears of relief, just the reassurance that Summer was on his side.

Chapter 5

A week had passed and all was good with the world, well, all was good with Simon and Summer. He hadn't heard from Teddy or Joseph but then he wouldn't, there was no need for them to get in touch, nothing had happened.

Summer came into the kitchen just as Simon was pouring a coffee. "I'm off to work now and I know you're driving your Mr Bay today, so be careful, and make sure you ring me before and after the pickup." She then kissed him on the cheek. His stomach was cramping, he put this down to drinking too much coffee on an empty stomach but deep down he knew it was also part to the fact that he was collecting Mr Bay in two hours. He did his post checks on the car but his heart wasn't in it. He double-checked his rear view mirror button, all was fine.

The drive over to Mr Bay's house was the same as it always was, and he was there in no time. His mind was just not on the job at all. The gates opened slowly as he said under his breath, "Well, here we go, it's all or nothing."

Mr Bay was waiting at the front door, he looked a bit on edge. "Morning, sir," Simon said as he opened the back passenger door. Mr Bay said not a word. "Where to, sir?"

He passed Simon two postcodes. "I have two meetings today, and as you know, I have you for three meetings the day after tomorrow and also the day after."

Simon nodded his head. "Yes, sir." The journey to the first meeting was through the busy town centre. No music was playing in the car, and again, Mr Bay seemed to be on edge. Simon drove up to a hotel called Chiswick Park, it was just outside a small town called Alum Rock. He dropped Mr Bay off at the front door and then parked at the back of the hotel and waited for his call. He then remembered he had to call Summer and not wanting to call her from his car because, let's be honest, he didn't know who was listening in. So he decided to take a walk around the grounds of the hotel. The smell of fresh-cut grass filled the air as he sat on the hotel bench. "Hi, Summer. I'm at the hotel."

"And are you okay?" Summer said as she closed the door to her office.

"Yes, I'm fine. I'm at the back of the hotel. Mr Bay has gone inside for a meeting. He said it will be at least two hours so I'm going to grab a bite to eat."

Summer told him to be careful and to ring her at the next hotel. The grounds of the hotel looked so beautiful, the flowers were in full bloom. There were even some rabbits on the lawn. He sat there eating his bacon panini, waiting for his call, and every now and then, he would break a piece off the panini to feed it to the birds. He was at the hotel for less than two hours, which meant it was a short meeting, when he got the call from Mr Bay to meet him at the front of the hotel. He put his half-eaten panini back into the bag and then placed it into his glove box. As he pulled around to the front of the hotel, Mr Bay was again outside waiting for him. "Are we going to the second postcode, sir?" Simon said as he put his seat belt on.

"Yes, Simon, but this is not a hotel, it's a supermarket." This was another one of Mr Bay's businesses that ran under the green leaf company. He had seven shops dotted around the UK.

As Simon set off out of the main gate of the hotel, Mr Bay answered his phone. Simon pulled his mirror down as always, pushing the button as he did so. He was able to pick up on particular parts of the conversation. "Yes, has the boat set sail yet? Port of Amsterdam. Yes, we can do that. When will he arrive in Cobh? I will arrange the car with trade plates. Stranraer, yes. I will arrange the hotel in Kendal. Let me know ASAP, keep in touch." Mr Bay then put his phone on the seat next to him as Simon pulled the mirror back up and touched the button at the same time. His second meeting was only a matter of minutes away. It was down a back street and a far cry away from the hotel he had just come from. Simon stayed with his car, not that anybody would do anything to it, he just felt it was the right thing to do. He watched Mr Bay go into the shop, and then Simon locked the car from the inside and then finished his now somewhat cold panini. Time was now getting on, he looked across into the main window of the supermarket just to see if Mr Bay was any nearer to finishing his meeting. He had seen Mr Bay putting an envelope into his briefcase. Unknown to Simon, Mr Bay's green leaf supermarket company was also a cover for his illegal money lending business. Simon watched as Mr Bay argued with the person at the counter. He was now seeing a side to Mr Bay that he had never seen before. The person looked frightened and by his body language, he seemed to be very apologetic. Mr Bay slapped him across the face, and then took his briefcase from the counter and walked towards the front door. Simon looked forward as if to say he hadn't seen anything. He didn't want to raise any suspicion to himself. Mr Bay got into the back of the car.

"Where to, sir?" Simon said as he looked into the rear view mirror.

"Nowhere yet, I need to make a phone call." The car ignition was turned off. Simon knew he couldn't push the button without the ignition being on, he had to think quickly.

"Sir, do you mind if I start the engine? It will stop the car from misting up."

Mr Bay looked up at him. "Of course not, please do." Simon coolly started his engine, then pulled his rear view mirror down, pushing the button as he did so. Mr Bay was furious, he was going on to the person on the other end of the phone about how he thought he was being conned out of money and then he said, "Get yourself down here and sort him out." He then put his phone away. "Right, Simon, let's go home." It was a nice drive back, Mr Bay was his normal self once again. He asked Simon how things were going at home and what he was getting up too, and how the business was doing. Simon had to remind himself what he was really like and the fact that he reigned down a living terror to anyone who would cross him.

That evening, Simon and Summer were sat watching television when they heard a ping from their laptop. They both knew who it was from, but Summer was the one who opened it. This part was all new to her. "It's giving you a promotional code. Simon wrote down the code and explained to Summer how it worked. He said it was too late to do anything now and would ring it through first thing in the morning. The following morning soon came around and Summer was up before Simon which was unusual. There was a lot on her mind, she wanted this sorted out just as much as Simon did. She placed his laptop on his knees in bed. Simon had to explain to her that he just couldn't jump online at this time in the morning because there wouldn't be anybody there. But truth be known, he didn't really know. It was just as new to Simon as it was to Summer. He waved Summer off to work that morning as usual and then went into his garage to check on the car. He had an easy day ahead and no Mr Bay to contend with. That would be tomorrow and the day after but it still didn't stop him thinking about what was to come. He was all set to go now and the highlight of his day was taking some rich old lady shopping. But he had enough time for one last coffee and to get in touch with the fat club. Making sure the door was locked, he rang Jessica Green.

"Good morning, FAT CLUB. How may I help?" Simon gave his promotional code and then his own code number.

"Ah, good morning, Mr Rodgers. I'm putting you through to Teddy now."

"Good morning, Simon. Teddy here, hope you're well." Simon didn't have time to answer before Teddy interrupted him, "I have some information about the telephone conversation with Mr Bay." Simon was all ears. Teddy was now going to fill in the missing pieces to the conversation Mr Bay had in his car. The Kite is sailing from the port of Amsterdam to Southern Ireland to a port called Cobh. Mr Bay had also arranged money for him as he only had euros and he needed sterling plus his passport for the UK. He was also going to arrange a car with trade plates from one of his car sales businesses in Northern Ireland. That would get him over by boat to Stranraer, and from there, he would drive down to Kendal where he would be given instructions on what to do next.

Simon interrupted Teddy, "Can't you arrest him in Stranraer and have done with it?"

Teddy explained to him, "Yes, we could but we need to know who his target is. It's nearly over now, let's not rush in at the last fence. When are you seeing him again?"

"Tomorrow and the day after, I'm driving him down to Oxford."

"Right," Teddy said. "Let's hope we don't lose any vital information in the meantime. You're doing well, Simon, just stay with it, it's nearly over now."

The rest of Simon's day was spent on his feet. To say he was supposed to be driving the old lady around the shops was an understatement. He was actually the old lady's bag boy and by the end of the day, his feet were killing him, but she was paying the bill so did it matter? No, it didn't. Money is money as he would say. That evening, Simon made a meal for both himself and Summer, and they talked most of the night, and again, it was about what had gone on. This was the only way Summer could come to terms with the situation but at the same time, she was now looking at her husband in a different way. He had a different look about him, she felt he was living on the edge. It was exciting and she was now excited to be with him, to know him, he was her husband. She felt as if he was her secret agent, she thought of the times when they would both watched films together and Simon would say, "I can do that," or, "I taught him everything he knows." She looked at him and then hugged him, asking how he was feeling only to be told he was worried sick. It was a far cry from what she had just imagined. They both hugged each other that night, they hadn't hugged each other like that since the holiday, and for some reason, she now felt safe in his arms.

The following morning, his phone alarm woke them both up. They both had fell into a deep sleep as soon as their heads hit the pillow. They talked over breakfast which they hadn't really done before and then it was time for Summer to make a move. Simon waved her off as she drove down the drive.

It wasn't long before he was all set to go as well. All his checks were done including the check on the button on his rear view mirror. He had checked that at least four times before setting off. He once again pulled up to the gates of Mr Bay's house, they opened slowly as he drove up to the front of the house and then waited. It was only a minute or two before Mr Bay opened the front door, his wife was at his side. She kissed him on the cheek and then waved at Simon. He couldn't help but notice that Mr Bay had his overnight bag with him. Mr Bay explained as he put his bag into the boot of the car. "I have three meetings and it looks like it could run into a late night or possibly the third meeting will have to be an early morning. Is that okay?"

Simon had to think quickly. "I can't see there being a problem with that, sir. Let's get you to your first meeting and I will make arrangements for my overnight stay." Simon was always prepared for the unexpected and always had his own overnight bag in the foot well. The drive over to Oxford ran like a dream. Mr Bay was quite talkative, there was no phone calls on the way down. All in all, it was a pleasant journey.

Simon arrived at his first postcode, it was the Lord Nelson. The parking was limited so Simon dropped Mr Bay off at the front doors and then parked down a side street, and waited for his call. He was now at a loose end. He called Summer and told her everything was going okay but he would have to stay out that night, and as she knew that was normal, she told him to be careful and make sure to ring her first thing in the morning. Two hours passed and Simon got his call. Mr Bay was now ready for his pickup. Simon pulled up to the hotel where Mr Bay was standing outside waiting for him. No sooner had he got in the car, his phone rang. Simon pulled his mirror down and touched the button as he did so. He could tell by his conversation that it was Mr Bay's wife. He listened in as much as he could to try and pick up as much information as possible.

"Yes, dear. We're still going. I'll meet you at Heathrow. Yes, I have the tickets in my case, you have to be at the airport for twenty two hundred hours. I know it's a late flight but that's because I have to be here for these meetings. Once they are finished, I'll take you on a nice holiday. Yes, dear, make sure you go to the right gate number, the flight number is YH6356, and don't be late." He put his phone down and Simon pulled his mirror back up again, pushing the button as he did so.

"Off on holiday, sir?"

"Yes, my wife has said I'm working too hard."

"Good for you, sir." Simon followed the next postcode. This time, it was a small pub down the back streets of Oxford. Once again, he had no choice but to stay with his car as Mr Bay sat in one of the back rooms of the pub. A minder watched the doorway, nobody had seen this side of Mr Bay's seedy operations, and just as he started the meeting, his phone rang. It was the Kite and he seemed somewhat agitated.

"You have a ghost in your organisation and they know I'm here."

"How do you know that?"

The Kite answered, "Do you think I am stupid? I spotted them at Stranraer but lost them just outside Dumfries. I'm telling you, someone is following me they know I'm in England."

Mr Bay told him, "Look, this is what I'm paying you for, just get the job done."

"I am a man of my word and a man with a reputation for seeing a job through but the price has just gone up. This should have been a plain and simple in and out job, but now the price has gone up another five thousand euro, take it or leave it."

Mr Bay cut to the chase, "Just get the job done and get it done now." And with that, he put the phone down.

"Right, gentleman, where were we?" The five of them ironed out their differences about the pilfering within the organisation and came to the conclusion that they should be made an example off. Mr Bay then called the meeting to an end as he now had more serious issues to consider. His head was now all over the place, he hadn't told anyone else, he had kept it to himself or so he thought. He walked outside and got back into the car using his phone scanner.

"Take me to the last postcode, please, Simon." This meeting was the most important one of all. This was what Mr Bay called new blood. These were up and coming gangs, young people with ambition and this was very important to him. The journey was going to take about an hour or so as it was the other side of Oxford, just on the outskirts. Simon sensed there was something wrong, but Mr Bay was deep in thought. He thought it could be his wife but why would it be her and anyway, he never ever talked about anything to do with his work. His close men that he called his coordinators, he knew they were loyal to him and he knew they would lay down their lives for him. He trusted them impeccably and he had just left them at the last pub. Simon was now on his way to another pub but it was like something he had never seen before. The windows were boarded up and two young men stood at the doorway. He pulled up slowly to the front of the pub.

Mr Bay said, "I'll be an hour maybe two if all goes well." Mr Bay walked over to the front door where the two young men searched him before letting him pass. One of the men came up to Simon and tapped on his car window. Simon somewhat reluctantly dropped his window.

"Yo, bro, nice machine. It's yours, bro?" Simon nodded his head. "How fast it go, bro? Bet it fast, innit?" Simon nodded his head again. "Respect, bro. No one will lay fingers on your machine here, bro." He then walked back over to the door. Mr Bay was just sitting down at the table, three young men sat opposite him, and a further six stood around him wearing what looked like Halloween mask and hoodies.

"Okay, gentleman, you can call me Mr Bay." The three of them laughed at him as they took another drink of Dalmore. Then, one of them pushed the bottle over to him.

"Want a drink?" The chrome stag's head on the bottle glistened in the dim light. Mr Bay couldn't believe these thugs were drinking Dalmore whisky, what a waste. The gang leader asked Mr Bay what could he do for him.

Mr Bay put both his hands palms down on the table and explained the situation. "I am now your new contact. Your old contact has ceased to exist for whatever reason which is not my concern. I am now your new supplier for the organisation."

The gang leader asked, "I don't know you, bro. I don't trust you." Mr Bay took the bottle of Dalmore from the table and had a drink from the bottle. This was a sign of respect for the gang leader.

He then said, "I will be here tomorrow evening which will give you time to contact your man to check me out."

And with that said, Mr Bay pushed his chair back, and as he did so, one of the six thugs opened the door and shouted to the two men outside, "Is it clear, bro? He's coming out."

One of the men outside then walked over to Simon's car. "Your man's coming out, bro." Simon nodded his head and then got out of his car to open the back door just as Mr Bay came out. Simon drove out of the back streets and back into what he called civilisation. Mr Bay drank two small bottles of water to take the taste of the Dalmore away whilst cursing the gang leader.

"These young men today have no respect." Simon looked in his mirror and agreed with him only because it had just terrified him. They drove back into Oxford into the city centre. The evening city lights reflected back off Simon's car as he eventually came to a stop outside the Majestic Hotel.

Simon turned to Mr Bay. "What time would you like to be collected tomorrow, sir?"

"I'm not sure, Simon," Mr Bay said. "It's been a long night as you will agree. I would think about two o'clock would be fine. I shouldn't need you until then but I will ring you if there's any change."

"Okay," Simon said as he got out of the car opening the back door for him. Again, Simon waited till Mr Bay had gone into the hotel before driving away to one of the many budget hotels he stayed in.

Mr Bay had settled down for the night and was on the phone to his wife when he received an incoming call. "I have a call on the other line, dear, let me answer it and I'll ring you back."

"Hello," it was the Kite.

Mr Bay sat down on the end of the bed. "Did you get the brown envelope with the information regarding the individual?"

"Yes," the Kite said he had been looking at the pictures of the woman he was about to assassinate, she was an activist for political and social change which would be damaging for Mr Bay and his organisation if she went ahead with her talk. He had arranged for the assassination of her for the day after he and his wife left the United Kingdom. The Kite still had concerns about the ghost in Mr Bay's organisation and Mr Bay was still adamant the ghost was not on his side. He was convinced it was to do with the Kite.

They exchanged words for five minutes or so before the Kite asked about Mr Bay's driver. "What driver? Do you mean Simon?"

The Kite asked if that was his name. "Do you know him well?"

"Yes," Mr Bay said. "I've known him for two years. He's a good man."

The Kite interrupted him, "Yes but how well do you actually know him?"

Mr Bay couldn't answer the question. He didn't know him that well, at the end of the day, he was just his driver. Mr Bay dropped his phone on the bed and put his head in his hands just for a moment. He could hear the Kite on the phone calling for him. "Are you there, are you there?"

Mr Bay picked the phone up. "Yes, I'm here. What do you suggest we do?"

The Kite said to him, "I need to speak with your driver. I need to know who was tailing me. What time do you fly tomorrow?" Mr Bay told him what time they were flying and the time he's meeting his wife, and at what airport. He told him what terminal and the gate number. He told him everything, he just wanted to get to the bottom of this as he was now getting paranoid. The other line on his phone started to ring.

"Look, I have to go. You have all the details now. I'll see you tomorrow." The line went dead and then the second line came in.

"Yo, Mr Bay, you check out, bro. We see you at three at the pub. Okay with that, bro?"

Mr Bay was quite sharp with his response, there was too much happening around him. The hotel room felt like it was closing in on him. "Three o'clock it is. I will see you there." And then, he put the phone down, he then rang Simon. "I've just had the call and I need to be at the meeting for three o'clock so you need to be at the hotel for two." He didn't wait for a response, he just put the phone down. Simon sat at a small writing table in his room, just looking into the mirror on the wall. Something wasn't right, it just didn't feel right. He didn't sleep that night. He tossed and turned for most of the time, he rang Summer and even she couldn't reassure him. He didn't let on he was worried, that was the last thing he wanted to do. As the dawn broke, he pulled back the curtains, it was now going to be a long day.

Chapter 6

There was no hot water that morning, so Simon had to brave the cold water, but once he was in the shower, it wasn't that bad. He called down to reception for breakfast in his room. He just couldn't face the hustle and bustle of the breakfast room downstairs. He was just doing his tie when there was a single tap on the door. It was the maid with his breakfast, the smell of her perfume filled the room. He wanted to ask her what it was called but thought it was unwise. The sun was just breaking through the trees as he sat at the window seat just watching the world go by, just having some me time. Mr Bay's meeting wasn't until the afternoon which gave Simon the full morning to do what he wanted. But for Mr Bay, things were definitely different. He had the world on his shoulders, not only did he have the meeting to attend, he also had the Kite on his back and a ghost somewhere in the organisation. They both watch television in their rooms but there worlds were so far apart. Time ticked on, and it wasn't long before he got his text from Mr Bay, 'Ready when you are.' That's all it said. Simon picked up his jacket and paid his bill on the way out. He texted Summer to say he would definitely be home and would see her later. Eventually, he pulled up to a slow stop out the Majestic Hotel and moments later, Mr Bay appeared at the main door. Simon took his bag and put it in the boot.

"Right," Mr Bay said. "Let's get this over with and then I can go on holiday with my wife." Simon drove back out of Oxford and back down the side streets. The nearer he got the pub, the dirtier the streets got. Once again, Simon pulled up outside the pub. The two same men stood outside, the man he had seen yesterday put his hand up to him. In a strange way, Simon felt safe.

Mr Bay got out of the car saying to Simon, "Give me two hours, that should do it." He then waited at the door and then followed one of the men from inside into the back room. Even though it was around mid-afternoon, the place was still dark inside. He sat at the same table and in the same place as yesterday. The same three men were sat at the same place waiting for him, the same six men stood around the room.

Although Mr Bay couldn't tell who was who because they still had same Halloween masks as yesterday. Mr Bay took control straight away. "Well, have you been in touch with your man? I believe you have, and you now know who I am."

"Yes," the gang leader nodded his head.

Mr Bay continued, "Are we then in agreement with my credentials?" Again, the gang leader nodded his head. "Okay, then this is how it will work. You still get your supply and it comes into you the same way. But it comes in under my guidance and for that, it goes up ten percent." The whole place was in an uproar. Mr Bay leaned back into his chair and waited. He now knew they wouldn't touch him, he had the safety of the main supplier. He waited and then the gang leader put his gun on the table. Mr Bay looked at it, then looked at the gang leader. "So we have a deal, do we? Only I do have a plane to catch."

The gang leader stood up. "You best do right by me, bro, or I comes for you and yours."

Mr Bay stood up to challenge him. "First of all, I'm not your bro. My name is Mr Bay and that's what you will call me. Secondly, never put your gun on the table in front of me, unless you intend to use it." The gang leader picked it up and then put it into the back of his pants. Mr Bay once again took control. "So with that, are we now done, gentleman?"

Simon sat in the car waiting when he heard one of the men at the door shout out, "He's coming out." Mr Bay then appeared as Simon opened the back door for him and then nodded at the men on the door. Now that was all over, he drove down the back streets for the last time. It was just so depressing but then they were soon back out on to the busy roads of Oxford.

"Where to, sir?"

Mr Bay sat back into his seat. "To the airport, please, Simon."

"Yes, sir." Oxford to Heathrow was only about an hour's drive away and that would get him there to early.

Mr Bay said, "Take the back roads." That would get him there for around six o'clock. He rang his wife to let her know to meet him in the V.I.P lounge. Simon pulled up at the short stay car park and then helped Mr Bay with his bag, the rest of his luggage was coming with his wife. Simon walked into the check in area as Mr Bay walked off in front of him. He had seen somebody he knew. He then watched as Mr Bay shook his hand and then patted him on the back, and then called Simon over, "Simon, this is one of my business associates. His flight has got in early. Would you mind dropping him off in Oxford on your way home?"

Simon said, "That would be fine. Do you have any bags, sir?"

"I just have the one case." He took it from him.

He then said to Mr Bay, "Have a good holiday, sir." As he turned to go back to his car, he asked the man if he had been waiting long.

"No, not really," he said. They got to the car where Simon put his case in the boot, and noticed there was no flight tags on his case and there was a price tag still attached to it. As they drove away from the airport, Simon tried to make conversation but it was very awkward. He noticed he had a strange accent but couldn't quite put his finger on it. Simon asked his name.

"Abraham," he said. He then asked Simon what his name was.

"My name is Simon."

The next hour of the journey was quite tense. Abraham had ask him how long he had worked for Mr Bay and how did he meet him. Simon asked him questions but what was more worrying for Simon was the way Abraham looked. His face was long and thin, his complexion was pale to the point of nearly being grey. His eyes were a pale blue and his blonde hair fell down the right side of his face. He gave Simon directions to the house just as his phone rang. Something told Simon it just didn't look right. He pulled his mirror down and pushed the button.

Abraham asked him, "Why have you just done that?"

"What?"

"Why did you pull your mirror down?"

Simon explained, "Mr Bay always insisted I pull my mirror down when he used his phone, it's just habit. I can put it back up if you insist." Thankfully for Simon, it worked. Abraham told him to leave it. For the next five minutes, Simon tried to pick up on parts of the conversation.

"Yes, all is good. No, I am asking questions. Yes, I will. If he is, I will let you know. Of course, I will, I never leave loose ends." Simon was coming to the end of his journey when he realised where he was. It was the property Mr Bay had bought. "I can tell by the look on your face, Simon, you have been here before." Simon nodded his head. Abraham put his hand on Simons shoulder. "Would you mind getting my case from the boot please? Simon reluctantly carried his case up the path to the front door and then he felt something being pushed into the side of his back. Unknown to him, it was a Beretta. "Do as I say or I will shoot you in the back and one in your head as you fall. You have my word on that." Abraham gave him the key to the front door. "Go inside and turn right into the kitchen." Simon did as he was told. Once he was in the kitchen, Abraham told him to kneel down in front of the radiator. He then passed him a pair of handcuffs. "Put them on and around the radiator pipe." Abraham then placed a pillowcase over his head. Simon was shaking with fear, his breathing was erratic. Abraham placed his gun to his head, Simon held his breath as Abraham moved the gun away. "Now I have your attention. Who are you?" Simon didn't know what to say. Abraham put the gun back to his head. "I will say again, who are you?"

"I don't know what you mean. I don't know what to say." There was no sound or movement for five minutes or so. Simon turned his head to the side to try and listen. Had Abraham gone? Was he now on his own? The gun was once again pushed to his head.

"Who are you?"

Simon shouted, "My name is Simon Rodgers."

By this time, the penny had dropped for Simon. He now knew the man with the gun to his head was the Kite. Again, five minutes passed. Simon could hear what sounded like a phone being taken apart, it was his phone.

Joseph burst into Teddy's office. "Simon's gone dark."

Teddy pushed back his chair and stood up. "What?"

Joseph said it again not that Teddy didn't hear the first time, "He's gone dark."

Teddy sat back down. "Where's his car and do we still have a tracker on it?"

"Yes we do," Joseph waited.

"Okay. Is Robyn still on his tail?"

"Yes, sir."

"Right. I want you to meet up with him and tell him to do whatever it takes to get Simon out of there alive."

Simon's breathing was becoming even more erratic, the sweat was now running down his face and into his eyes. "Are you the ghost?"

Again, Simon shouted, "I don't know what you mean. My name is Simon Rodgers."

"No, you are the ghost, it can only be you. You are the ghost." The Kite pushed the gun hard into Simons head. He knew this was now getting serious. All he could think about was his wife, Summer. It seemed strange that only yesterday he was saying goodbye to her but now realising he may never see her again, he felt the pressure of the gun against his head knowing it could go off at any moment. The pillowcase was now getting wet with the condensation from his heavy breathing.

Teddy picked up his phone on the first ring. It was Jessica. "It's Joseph on the line for you, sir, putting him through."

"Go on, Joseph."

"Sir, we have the location of Simon's car."

"Good," Teddy said. "Where are you now, Joseph?"

"We are travelling with a blue light on the motorway. We're about one hour away, sir."

"Good. Tell Robyn he must do his best to protect Simon from harm and tell him he must go in with a Shoot to Kill. I want the Kite out of the way once and for all. Let me know what the outcome is ASAP."

Simon had the pillowcase over his head for nearly two hours and was trying to stay positive, but although it had only been two hours, it felt like a lifetime. The Kite was forcing the gun between his shoulder blades. "I will do this until you tell me what I need to know and my patience is now wearing thin. I could finish you now if I choose." Simon then felt a hand being placed softly on his shoulder and then the pillowcase was pulled from his head. He turned his head to where the Kite was standing, his cold blue eyes stared down at him. "It's unfortunate for you, Simon, and it's not your fault that you have been pulled into this situation. But where are the people that put you up to this? Where are they now you need them to save you?" I will tell you, Simon, they are nowhere to be seen. They will leave you here to die. You are a good man, you have a wife at home waiting for you, so why protect these people who have put you in this place? All I need is the person who has put you here. Tell me, you are the ghost, aren't you, Simon?"

Simon looked at him for a minute or so and then put his head down. "I don't know what you mean. I just drive for Mr Bay." The Kite slapped him across the back of his head and then put the pillowcase over his head once again. Simon knew the longer he kept quiet, the longer he had a chance of staying alive.

Joseph and Robyn turned off their blue light as they pulled off the motorway. They then drove down the A road that by passed Oxford town centre. Joseph looked at the tracking display on the dashboard. "Simon's car is nearby. It's literally the next turning off, and then it's two streets away." As they turned down the last street, they could see Simon's car was parked on the left hand side of the road, but they weren't sure as to which house it was. Robyn turned his lights off as he pulled over to the side of the road, and then they both sat and waited as they looked across at the two houses, but which one was Simon in. They were now losing time, but then their waiting paid off. A light came on in the front room of the house next door, the occupier closed the curtains and then turned the light off. That's what they were waiting for, now they both knew where Simon was, but now they had to get to him before it was too late. Joseph realised he needed to get to the front window without drawing too much attention to himself.

Robyn asked, "How are we going to play it?"

"We play the oldest trick in the book." Joseph opened the paper recycle bin of the house. He then took out a hand full of door-to-door leaflets. Robyn waited at the sidewall of the house, checking the side entrance. He gave a thumbs up sign as Joseph moved up to the front window of the house. The front room was in darkness but the door to the hallway was slightly open. A shimmer of light lit up the carpet near the door. He then moved to the front door, and looked through the frosted glass. There was no light that he could see. This told him this was now in their favour as he now knew the Kite would close the first door and then open the second one. This would keep anything out of sight from the front door so, therefore, Simon had to be in the kitchen or the back room.

Joseph put the leaflets under an empty milk bottle for safekeeping, and moved to Robyn at the sidewall of the walkway. They both needed to know which room Simon was in at the back of the house. Joseph stayed at the side of the house while Robyn made his way to the back. After a short time, Robyn had gotten to the back gate of the property. He had manoeuvred his way past the rubbish that had accumulated over the months and he now had a gate lock to contend with. A rusty bolt that took some doing to open without any noise, he was now at the back of the house. He could see there were two windows, one of them had the light on. He took out his phone from his pocket, and slowly put it to the corner of the window, and then pressed the video recorder remaining in a crouched position for about two minutes. He needed to get as much information as possible, he now knew he had to be very careful to retrace his steps to get back to Joseph.

It was going to be a long night. Joseph and Robyn stood side by side but facing each other. This technique was widely use in surveillance so one could look down the side of the walk way whiles the other looked up to the front of the house. Robyn played the video footage to Joseph and they both agreed it wasn't looking good for Simon. They both had seen how the Kite was hitting him around his back. He was handcuffed to the radiator and had a pillowcase over his head. Joseph said, "He's in a bad way. If he's had to endure what he has gone through for the past few hours, then if he hasn't already talked, he soon will. We do really need to make our move now or we're not going to save him, and let's be honest, if Simon has talked, we then need to know who to. Our cover may already be blown."

Robyn said, "We already know he's the Kite." The plan was for Joseph to knock on the front door and then hand the Kite some leaflets. They had thought about jumping him at the front door but then thought there odds would be greater if they did it this way. Robyn explained to Joseph that the backdoor was unlocked and the door to the dining room was wedged open. He knew there would be a way of getting behind it and waiting. They both set their phones to vibrate in four minutes. Robyn made his way back round to the back of the house and waited. His phone vibrated in his hand as he watched from the corner of the window. He could see the Kite move to the dining room door. He watched as the Kite stopped and looked back at Simon. Robyn moved back into the darkness to avoid any detection. He then watched as the Kite make his way to the front door.

Now was his opportunity to make his move. He slowly opened the door to the kitchen, and once inside, could hear Joseph talking at the front door. He slowly moved across the kitchen, making sure he didn't startle Simon. The last thing he wanted was Simon getting upset and blowing his cover. He managed to get behind the dining room door and then pulled the door up to himself. Joseph had done his bit. He had kept the Kite at the front door for as long as he possibly could have done. Then there was a silence as the Kite closed the door behind him. Robyn could hear the Kite's footsteps on the laminated flooring in the front room as he walked back to the kitchen. He also could hear Simon trying to control his pain, Simon felt the gun on his neck yet again. "It looks like your friend has come to rescue you with his feeble attempt to pass as a door salesman, but you had your chance and you didn't take it and now you have to go." Simon closed his eyes and thought of his wife, Summer. He didn't say a word, he wasn't going to give the Kite the satisfaction. "So long," the Kite said as he put the gun to Simons head. Two shots were fired with a muzzled sound from a silencer. The weight on Simon's head was overpowering. Was this it, was he now going to die? It was only a matter of seconds and the weight was lifted from him. He could hear the sound of something being dragged away from him and then he felt a hand on his head. He pulled back away from it.

"It's okay, Simon. It's okay." Simon knew that softly spoken voice. The pillowcase was pulled from his head as he looked to see who it was. His eyes welled up when he knew he was finally safe. Robyn sat down next to him putting his hands on Simon's shoulders. He told him to breathe, because he was going into shock. The back door to the kitchen was pushed open as Robyn raised his gun to cover the door. Simon knew the gun had been fired by its smell of the gun as it passed his head. Robyn held his aim, it was Joseph. He dropped down his gun to his side.

"He's in the living room, it's done. Can you get me the key to the handcuffs?" Joseph tossed the key to him and then went back into the living room to check the body. Simon asked if he was dead.

"Yes," Robyn said. "He's dead."

Simon put his head down. "I'm glad, he's dead. I'm glad." He was now beginning to breathe normally, Robyn had taken the handcuffs off him but still had him sat on the floor with his back to the wall for support. He sat with him whilst Joseph rang in for a body collection and informed Teddy that the Kite was no more. The collection was there within the hour as well as a medical nurse to check over Simon. Robyn had arranged for himself to take Simon home and to have him checked out on the way. Meanwhile, Joseph stayed with the body and organised the clean-up.

It was a lovely evening as Simon walked out of the house. It was a far cry from what had just happened. He got into the back of Robyn's car as the medical nurse sat next to him. She asked him some questions about how he was feeling and examined the lumps on his head. After a short time, she gave him the all clear, which was a big relief to him. He sat back into his seat and looked out of the side window, and even though he was looking out, he wasn't looking at anything. It was all just one big blur, everything was unclear to him. He had been so close to death but yet felt so alive.

"Are you okay? It looked like you were away with the fairies then."

Simon turned his head away from the car window. "Yes, I'm alright."

Robyn told him what the plan was, "We're going to drop your car off back to you in the next couple of days. What are you going to tell your wife?" Simon looked at him through the rear view mirror. He could see Robyn's eyes and in a way, Simon knew that Robyn had guessed that Summer was already in the picture. They were getting closer to Simon's house when Robyn said to him, "You must never talk to anyone about what happened tonight." Simon turned his head back to the side window and nodded. His journey was now coming to an end, and so was his ordeal. Robyn pulled up outside his house, all the lights where off, it was total darkness in the dead of the night except for one solitary side light in the bedroom.

He got out of the car and stood on his driveway, looking up at the night sky. He heard Robyn say, "You're safe now, we will be in touch." Simon put his hand up, he didn't turn round, he just walked up the drive to the front door of his house. His hands still trembling slightly from his ordeal. To his surprise, Summer opened the door as he looked back at Robyn's car turning the corner at the bottom of the road. He felt a pull on his arm as she pulled him in from the front door. Tears were rolling down her cheeks.

"Is it over? Please tell me it's over."

Simon closed the front door. "It's over."

Because of Simon's help Mr Bay was arrested at the airport, and later, convicted for his crimes which were manslaughter supplying drugs and money laundering. He ended up with a twenty-five years' sentence with all his assets seized.

His wife moved back to her family in Argentina to avoid any confrontation with Mr Bay's past.

All the gang leaders were arrested and their businesses closed down.

The Kite never got to ring Mr Bay to say the ghost was Simon, so therefore, Simon was in the clear.

The Kite's body was cremated and his ashes were scattered at an unknown location. As far as anyone in the underworld knew, it was presumed he had gone into hiding.

Three months had now passed and Simon's business had gone from strength to strength. Mainly because Teddy had put a lot of business Simon's way as a show of appreciation for what he had done for the fat club, and to make things even better. They were both now sat on a plane flying above the clouds bound for Casablanca, courtesy of the fat club, when the air stewardess stopped at Simon's seat. "Mr Rodgers."

Simon sat up in his seat. "Yes, that's me."

Summer took off her headphones just as the stewardess said, "I have a bottle of champagne for you, sir, and I have been instructed to give you this envelope."

The champagne was poured as Simon opened the envelope. "It's from Teddy."

Summer stopped Simon in his tracks. "It better not be anything to do with that fat club. You better tell them no." Simon told her it was just a thank you for all he had done. Summer put her head phones back on and closed her eyes.

Simon started to read the letter which said,

'Hello, Simon, hope you and your lovely wife, Summer, are well. Please enjoy your holiday and the champagne, and please contact me on my number when you get home.'

Simon looked at Summer. She was fast asleep. He then put the letter into his inside pocket and as he looked out of his window, he could see himself smiling in the reflection.

Chapter 7

The holiday was now over and it had already become a distant memory, and all they had to show for two weeks in the sun was a suntan and of course, lots of pictures on their phones. Simon was now sat at Teddy's desk, a far cry from the bar in the Palm Bay Hotel where they had long rum and black drinks. But now that was all over and Simon was sitting in front of Teddy once again. "You have a new girl on the front desk, Teddy. Where's Jessica?"

"Ah, Jessica Green. Well, she's been moved up into another department."

Simon looked at Teddy. "Why?"

Teddy said, "It's best we don't ask. Anyway, Simon, how is your lovely wife, Summer, and how was your holiday in Casablanca?" Simon told him all about the hotel and that Summer looks even more gorgeous with a suntan.

Now Teddy had broken the ice once again, it was now time to get down to business. First of all, he thanked Simon again for all the hard work he had put in on catching the Kite.

Simon interrupted, "You mean getting him killed." It was still a sore point for him.

Teddy took control again, "Simon, you must understand it was him or you and it is you that is sitting here in this room with me, now is that not so." Simon nodded his head. "Good," Teddy said as he opened his file. "Things have moved on in the short time you've been away. Not only did we manage to get Mr Bay with your help, but we now have a good chance of getting the king pin as well."

Simon looked at him. "Right, and this is where I get up and walk out of this office."

Teddy picked up his phone. "Wait one minute, Simon, please just one minute."

The lady on the front desk answered, "Yes, Teddy, can I help you?"

"Yes, Rose, can we have tea for two?" Simon looked at Teddy once again. He had been here once before and he thought to himself, *Look where that got me.*

The lift door opened and Rose pushed the tea trolley into the room. "You know Simon, don't you?"

Rose, "Yes, sir, we met in reception."

Simon said, "Hello."

Once again, as Teddy made tea, the lift door silently closed as Teddy opened his file. "Right, Simon, please let me tell you where we are while you enjoy your tea." Teddy began to read out the information from the file and not once did he look up at Simon. "It seems that our man Mr Slimm is the head of the organisation and the fat club would like to take him down. We already have our Mr Bay behind bars and he won't be out for a long time, but if we could get Mr Slimm then that would put the final nail in the coffin so to speak."

Simon was at this time already hooked, he took a sip of his tea. "And where do I come in?"

Teddy now looked up at him. "We would like you to be our Mr Bay. There's a lot to go over with you if you decide to take it on, I would understand if you want to walk away from this, and I would understand if you did."

Simon put his cup of tea down on Teddy's desk. "How much can you tell me before I am fully committed?"

Teddy pushed the file to one side. "Simon, as you know we sent you on holiday to Morocco as part of our appreciation for your work. Well, it wasn't all true. Yes we did send you both on holiday but you both picked something up for us, and before I go on, can I just say you and your wife were never in any danger. You met Youssef, the hotel barman, did you not?"

Now he had Simon's attention. Simon now picked his cup up with both hands as not to show his nerves. "Yes I did, he's a very polite man."

"Yes, he is," Teddy said. "He's also our man. You had a Blue Lagoon cocktail, did you not?"

Simon once again put his cup down on Teddy's desk. "Look, where's this going?"

Teddy walked over to where the tea trolley was, taking Simon's cup from him. "I take it you have finished with your cup, Simon. You see, Simon, Youssef had some information he needed to get to us regarding Mr Slimm. I take it you have your phone on you with the photos of your holidays."

Simon took the phone from his pocket. "Yes, I do."

"And I take it you still have the photos on your phone, do you not?" Simon opened to the holiday folder. Teddy was now standing looking over Simon shoulder. "There he is, that's Youssef." Teddy then sat back down at his desk and picked up his phone. "Rose, can you come into my office and can you bring the scanner with you please?" It was only a minute or so, then the lift door opened and in walked Rose once again. This time with the scanner under her arm. She put it down on Teddy's desk and then stepped back, Teddy then turned it on. "Right, Simon. Open your picture folder to the one with you and your wife holding the cocktails." And there it was, Simon, Summer and the barman called Youssef. Teddy placed Simon's phone on the scanner and then pressed the mirroring button, and within seconds, it had been sent to Teddy's laptop. Simon then picked up his phone as Teddy said to him, "You must now delete all of your pictures with Youssef on them for security reasons." Teddy then got up from his desk and looked over Simon's shoulder as he did so. "Good, now that's done, and I now have the picture I need, I can now go more in-depth with the situation." Teddy told Rose that was all and that she could now go back to her desk, he then watched as the lift door closed.

Simon was now sat opposite Teddy at his desk, just sat there waiting, waiting for Teddy to say something whether it be good or bad but to Simon's astonishment, Teddy asked him a question that was going to put a completely different outlook on things. "Your wife, Summer."

"Yes, what about her?" he said.

Teddy looked into Simon's eyes, he had a way of making people sweat. It was as if he was going over in his head what he was going to say next. He said it again, "Your wife, Summer, she knew about what was going on, didn't she?"

Simon looked at him not sure about what to say. "Be very careful, Simon, how you answer my question. Think about what you're going to say next." Simon knew his cards were out on Teddy's desk, he knew the best way was to come clean.

"Yes, she knew."

"So why did you tell her after everything we had said?"

"I had to," Simon said. "You don't know what strain you put on my marriage. Summer thought I was having an affair so therefore I had to tell her, and to be honest, I couldn't have done it without her. She was and still is my rock."

Teddy looked at him again. "Robyn knew."

"What?" Simon said.

Teddy said it again, "Robyn had an idea that Summer knew about it, the night he was taking you home, and he reported it to me straight away. He had explained to me that you were prepared to die rather than give up the organisation you were working for. Was that right?" Simon nodded his head. "Summer must be a strong individual to know you were putting your life on the line, even though you your self didn't know you were in any danger till it was too late." Again, Simon nodded his head. Teddy got up from his desk and walked around the room rubbing his knee. "This damn war wound," he said as he laughed it off and as he did so, Simon laughed with him. But his laugh was a nervous one. "I would like to meet your wife, Simon."

Simon answered him straight away, "No, that's not going to happen."

Teddy sat back down at his desk still rubbing his knee. "That's better. So, Simon, when can I see you both together? It would be nice to put a face to the name."

Simon again said, "No, it's not going to happen."

"I'll tell you what we can do," Teddy said. "At least, let me book you a table at the Richmond, just for you two so you can have a talk. At least, do that for me. You see, Simon, I have a good judgement in people. After all, I believed in you, did I not? Anyway, it's time you got yourself home to your lovely wife, is it not? Let Rose know what date and time you want the Richmond for." Teddy then took him back down to reception. "Looking forward to seeing you and your wife soon, Simon. Rose, can you show Simon out?"

Simon's drive home was a somewhat hectic one, purely because of the time of day, but then he had all the time in the world. He had his own drivers now, three to be precise, so he only drove for special clients. The one's Teddy needed to keep an eye on, so a lot of his time was spent in his office at the back of the garage. He had just got on the motorway when he got an incoming call, it was Summer.

"Hello you," she said. "I'm on my way home. Where are you?" He told her he was on the motorway and would be home in about two hours. She didn't ask where he actually was, which was to his blessing, because if she had, then she would have known just where he had been and then there would have been eruptions. They both talked for about five minutes about nothing and then Summer said, "I'll see you when you get home, drive carefully."

As Simon drove through the heavy traffic, he thought about what Teddy had said. Then Simon realised that all his eggs were in one basket so to speak. A lot of his work was now through Teddy, and yes, he could pull out and go on his own again, but did he really want to go through all that again. Life was so easy now, and he was spending so much more time with Summer which was what he always wanted. It wasn't long before he was on the A road that took he through the town to this house. Home sweet home, it was that good feel factor as he pulled up on to his drive. Summer waved to him from the front living room window, Simon waved back at her as his garage door opened as he drove in.

"How's your day been?" Summer said as she poured a glass of wine for him.

"Yes, it's been an interesting day." He thought it best not to say anything about seeing Teddy because she was in such a good mood and after all, it was Friday night. It could wait till Saturday morning, they both woke up with sore heads that morning and they both put it down to too much Montepulciano.

Simon came straight out with it, "I called in at the fat club yesterday and Teddy was there." Summer was in a rage. Simon knew he had gone too far just by the look on her face.

"Why did you go and what on earth were you thinking of when you did it?"

Simon said, "I was compelled to do it. I had no choice but to go and see him, and anyway, everything's fine. I haven't been bamboozled into doing anything."

Summer looked at him. "Why do you get yourself into these situations? And then you find it difficult to get out of them. So what did he want you to do this time? The man has a nerve, I would like to give him a piece of my mind, I really would."

"Well, he's booked us a table at the Richmond in Highgate. All I have to do is let them know the date and the time."

Summer interrupted in excitement, "Do you know what the Richmond is? It is only the place to be seen in. It's only the place where the rich and famous go. Simon, are you sure he said the Richmond and it's the one in Highgate? You know what you're like for getting it wrong. I'll have to get a new dress."

Simon said under his breath, "Not another one. So is it okay to ring the fat club and tell them to book the table."

"Of course," summer said, still on a high.

"Okay, I'll ring them tomorrow and book it for a Friday night then."

Summer jumped in again, "No, it has to be a Wednesday night. That's the night when the rich and famous book for and that's the hardest time to get a table. So let's just see how good your Teddy friend really is." The penny have finally dropped for Simon. He now knew what Teddy was up to, Teddy was now dangling the carrot in front of Summer, and what a carrot it was going to be.

Saturday was quite a busy morning. Simon was in the process of selling his cars due to the high mileage and going down the lines of leasing, only because the way his company was expanding. Then in a business sense, it was the right thing to do, the time was now eleven o'clock. Simon walked out of his office and into the garage, he checked the large television screen which was also his monitoring and tracking system for his cars. He could see his cars were showing a green tick at the side of each car which meant all his cars were on the move, which again meant they were making money and that was sweet music to his ears. Just as he was going to turn away from the monitor, a small black square box on the top left-hand side of the screen flashed telling him there was someone outside. He pressed a button on the remote to activate the camera around the property. The image flashed up on the screen of Summer standing outside next to the garage door. She was waving at the camera, she then moved back away from the door as it opened.

"Hello you," she said as she walked in the garage. "Are you going to take me into your office?" This was it with Summer, she never took advantage of the situation. The fact that this was Simon's workplace and always asked to enter whenever she came down the path to see him. They both sat at Simon's desk. Simon moved his cup of coffee to the side away from any of the paperwork on his desk.

"What's to do, Summer? What's on your mind?" he said this because it was very rare that she ever came down into his business world. She left that side of the business to him, she just spent the money, not that she didn't make her own she just preferred to spend his. She was now looking at him with her cheeky smile, that knowing smile that was going to cost Simon money. "Go on, tell me what you're after. Don't beat about the bush, go on, just spit it out."

Summer shuffled in her seat. "Well," she said. "Are you done for the day?"

"Only if you are," she said with her cheeky knowing smile that always got her own way.

"Only if you are." Simon cut in. "Okay, what do you want?"

That was it, she had her own way again and Simon thought to himself, *She's caught me out again.*

As summer continued to say, "It's a lovely day so let's get you out for the rest of the day in the fresh air."

"Where to?" Simon said as he picked up his coffee.

That was it, that was Summer's opening. "I thought we could go to Maverick Mill. You know, the clothing outlet on the outskirts of town." Simon gulped on his coffee he knew this was going to cost him. The drive over to Maverick Mill was a pleasant one. Summer asked about Teddy and for the first time, she was genuinely interested in him. Simon told her Teddy was a Cambridge boy, he left with honours and soon followed in his father's footsteps by enlisting in the Grenadier Guards as a junior officer. He quickly moved up through the Regiment, and had a long and promising career but then it all went horribly wrong when he was shot in the knee on Manoeuvers. He was then placed behind a desk and a career change lead him down the path to the secret service where, once again, he made his mark until retirement knocked on his door. But then he was given a lifeline in the form of the fat club and here he is now. Summer was shocked at what Simon had told her and was now beginning to have some respect for him but that didn't mean she had forgiven him for what he had done to her Simon. They eventually pulled up on the car park of Maverick Mill and to say it was a big place was an understatement. It was the size of two football stadiums put together. Summer was the first one through the revolving door. Simon was hot on her heels. Once inside, Simon was amazed by the vast space, spinning clothes rails were placed in lines and garments filled them. The first row were your low cost every day garments, and the further in you walked, the more expensive it got. Needless to say, summer walked straight to the back of the mill to where all the designer clothing were. She homed in on the colour black, she always said it hides your lumps and bumps, and within minutes, Simon was two hundred and five pounds lighter in his pocket, and that was just the start. But then Summer would always buy him an Americano coffee which cost two pounds ten, big difference. They had been inside for just over four hours and was now walking back to the car, and once again, Simon was the bagman as Summer walked on ahead of him. Her hair blowing back in the light breeze. On the way back home, Summer asked Simon some more questions about the Fat Club. She was now getting more inquisitive about the organisation and about what they do.

The wind had picked up quite a bit as Simon pulled on to his drive. "It looks like rain," Summer said as she got her bags from the boot of the car. "But with all the sun we've had, a little rain will be good for the garden."

Simon opened the front door for her and then said, "I'll be in the office for about thirty minutes or so. I need to get hold of Rose at the Fat Club to book this table."

"Good afternoon, The Fat Club. How may I help?" Simon gave his code number and then waited. "Hello, Mr Rodgers. How may I help today?"

"It's about the table at the Richmond in Highgate. Teddy told me to ring you with a date and time." He waited for a response but there was none. "Hello, Rose, are you there?"

"Yes, I'm here, carry on."

"I would like book it for nine o'clock on the second of next month." Again, no response. He waited and thought to himself, is all the reception staff abrupt like this, just like Jessica she was the same, was this equality they had to have, she then came back on line.

"Mr Rodgers, I'm going to put you on hold."

"Hello, Simon. Teddy here, it looks like your wife has done her homework. Wednesday is only for the privileged few at the Richmond but I'm sure we can do something. Let me put you on hold for a minute or two." Simon sat at his desk and waited. "Hello, Simon. Teddy here again. We have you in on that date and time. You will be booked under John Hardmen and Lucy Hardmen, and your company is Hardmen advertising. This is one of our companies. Simon, the reason you're going in under that name is so we don't raise any suspicions because you must realise these are all wealthy people and I'm sure you will be able to talk Summer around to our way of thinking."

Simon asked for the names again as not to forget them and said, "Summer is her own person and will do what she thinks is right but I will do my best to point her in the right direction."

Teddy then said, "Well, I'm sure you'll do your best." Simon checked his bookings and then glanced at the television monitor as he passed on his way out of his garage. Summer had already poured a glass of wine for him which was placed on the island in the kitchen. It was a large glass which Simon took it as another reward for his shopping spree. He had no sooner sat down and put the television on when Summer walked in. She looked stunning, absolutely gorgeous. She was so giddy and excited about the evening to come.

"Well, what did he say, can he do it? Can he get us a table for that day?" Simon could see how excited she was. Summer waited for Simon's response.

"Yes, we have the booking, the tables booked."

She took a deep breath. "But is it booked for Wednesday?" She waited.

"Yes. Wednesday." Summer threw her arms around him in the excitement, she then straightened her black dress, and ran up the stairs and danced around her dressing room.

Teddy was sat at home when he got a phone call from Jack Triton. "Hello, Jack, how are you today?" Jack Triton was part of a two-man team in the decoding sector of the fat club, his partner, Oliver Edhog was away for the weekend and wouldn't be back till Monday so it was Jack's turn to man the phone for any important information that needed to be deciphered. They were both in their late twenties and both graduated from university with honours.

"Teddy, it's just to let you know the information on the cocktails you've been asking for is now ready for collection."

"Ah, very good, very good indeed. I look forward to tasting the drink."

Jack said, "I think you'll be pleasantly surprised with the results." Teddy put his phone down and picked up his glass of port. The cocktails Jack had been talking about was actually the code name for what was on the picture that Teddy had scanned off Simon's phone. Teddy had also arranged for Oliver and jack to be in his office on the Thursday, knowing that Simon's meal was on the Wednesday evening. This way, he would definitely have some information to fight his corner and hopefully, get Summer on board. As for Simon, he was already hooked. Summer, in his mind, was going to be the hard nut to crack.

Summer had calmed down and Simon was somewhat relieved as whenever she got giddy and whenever she had a sensation of whirling around, she would put the television on a music channel and turn the volume up as far as it could go, and this wasn't good for the neighbours, so Simon was quite relieved it hadn't gone that far. A quiet night in, that's what he really needed as tomorrow was going to be a busy morning for him.

Rise and shine, feet on the floor, it's another day. Well, for Simon it was. On the other hand, for Summer, it was her day off and that meant Simon was once again on tiptoe duty. His time today was going to be spent visiting his drivers as he now knew the leasing contract for the cars were now in their final stage. The plan was to talk to his drivers just to see if they were happy with everything. Simon's beliefs were that if his drivers were happy, then they were happy in their work. It was soon midday and he only had one more driver to see so he decided to pull over on a country lane lay-by. Summer had been asking him for days to order some fat burners. He still ordered from the Fat Club. He often thought he would get it a lot cheaper now he was a member of the club so to speak but Teddy would say we run a business here. He was on line when he got an incoming call on his car system. He knew the number, it was the fat club. "

Mr Rodgers, it's Rose. I have some information for you regarding your meal at the Richmond." Simon thought this women never has any time off, she's just like Jessica, it must be a condition of the job. That's no life, he thought.

"Go on, Rose."

"You will be collected by car at nineteen hundred hours."

Simon interrupted her, "That's a bit early, isn't it? That's giving us two hours to get there when it's only an hour away at that time in the evening."

Rose said it again, it was as if she hadn't heard a word he said. "The car will…"

"Yes, Rose. I heard the first time."

"Okay, Mr Rodgers. I bid you good afternoon."

And just like Jessica, she hung up on him. Simon was now home for the rest of the day. His last visit was all done and dusted. The evening was now his and Summer's. Wednesday soon came around. Summer had been in her dressing room for most of the afternoon but for Simon, he only needed forty minutes and he had done that an hour ago so he was helping himself to the wine when Summer walked into the kitchen. She looked so gorgeous, her below-the-knee black dress was so beautiful, she looked beautiful. Simon poured her a glass of red wine.

"Do we have time for this, Simon? The car should be here soon." And no sooner had she said it, a car horn sounded outside.

"Surely, that can't be our car. Why would they sound a horn?" Simon walked to the front window, it was a taxi. Summer followed him.

"It's a taxi," she said. "We can't go in a taxi, surely not." Simon calmed her down and then went outside.

"Mr Rodgers, I'm here to pick you up, sir."

Simon looked a bit confused. "It's okay, Mr Rodgers. All is fine, please ask your wife to come to the car and I'll explain on the way." Simon called Summer over to the car and reluctantly got in. This was not what she was expecting. Within ten minutes, they were off the estate and on the road that took them through the town when the driver said, "You're going to have a great evening."

Summer interrupted him, “Of course, we will. Turning up to the Richmond in a taxi that’s a good start.”

The driver looked at her through his rear view mirror. “Right, Mr Rodgers, you have been told you have been booked in as Mr and Mrs Hardmen, is that correct?”

Summer looked at Simon. “What’s going on?” Simon put his hand on her knee to reassure her.

The driver then said, “I’m taking you both to Hill Gate service station where there’s a car waiting for to take you to the Richmond.”

“Why?” Summer said. “Why are we doing this?” Simon knew he was in trouble again. The driver was looking at Simon through his rear view mirror waiting for Simon to explain but he didn’t.

The driver had no choice but to say, “This has to be low key from your home. As far as your neighbours are concerned, you’re just going out for a meal.” Summer looked at Simon again but got no response. “You will be met by the second driver shortly. He will explain everything to you both.”

The sun was just beginning to set for the evening as the taxi pulled to a stop at Hill Gate service station where a glossy black people carrier with blacked out windows was parked. The taxi driver opened his doors for them both as the driver of the black people carrier opened his. They both walked over to the driver not knowing what to expect. “Good evening, Mr and Mrs Rodgers. My name is Charles and I’m your driver for the evening. I’ve taken the liberty of opening a bottle of champagne for you, it’s waiting inside.” Simon helped Summer in and then sat down next to her. The side door automatically slid forward as they sat in the seats, they were in total darkness but only for a few seconds as a soft blue light illuminated the back of the cab. The mirrored glass window that separated the driver from them slid down to reveal the driver.

“As you know my name is Charles, I will be your driver for the evening. We are only twenty minutes away from the Richmond so I will be taking you both the long way around to get you there for twenty one thirty hundred hours. It’s fashionable to be late. I will make the necessary call and tell them you are caught up in traffic. This will then give the time to explain the evening for you both." They both sat back and enjoyed the champagne as Charles started to explain, "I think you already know we have had to book you in as Mr and Mrs Hardmen, is that correct?"

They both said yes at the same time but then Summer said, "Why?" She was the inquisitive one.

Charles explained why, "This was the only way we, The Fat Club could get you in. Any other night, there wouldn't have been a problem but on a Wednesday night, that is definitely a no for some one of your standing." Summer took another sip of her champagne and looked very sheepish but soon got over it. "Not that you don't deserve to be there, it's just that Wednesday night is for the rich and famous. So let me explain to you what's going to happen tonight. You will be the Hardmens for the evening, everything is paid for and on no circumstances do you pay for anything by cash. All we ask is that you don't overindulge, the food is not a problem but please take care with your drinks. We're not saying don't enjoy yourself, just be careful. Do not talk about your business, if anybody asks which they shouldn't but if they do, just tell them you're in advertising. When you arrive at the Richmond, you will be asked to hand in your mobile phones at the booking desk. This is because the Richmond has total privacy, there are no pictures taken or selfies for the media to get hold of. When you're ready to leave, let the desk know, they will notify me, I Will be at the door waiting for you. Any questions, I can help you with?" They both just looked at each other and then looked back at Charles. "Okay then, now everything has been made clear, just sit back and enjoy the rest of the journey with the champagne." The mirrored glass window slid back into position. Summer was now mesmerised as she sat in the back of the people carrier. The thick black leather seats hugged her as she sat, a thin blue rope light ran along the edge of the thick pile carpet, a mini bar was fitted behind the driver's window to the left hand side. This was something that Summer had only dreamed of. She'd seen this sort of thing on reality TV but never thought that she would get to ride in one. Charles's voice came over on car speakers, "the Richmond is five minutes away." through the privacy glass, they could see dim flashes of light as the people carrier pulled to a stop. Charles said, "Don't stop for anyone on your way in, the doorman will open the door as you get to it. Have a great evening."

Two red ropes on poles lined the way to the Richmond doors. There were about ten people with cameras flashing away every now and then. Summer would cover her eyes from the camera flash, she was loving the attention. The doorman opened the door for them and then closed quickly behind them. They were now in a small lobby. A person stood behind the reception desk, "Mr and Mrs Hardmen."

"Yes," Simon said.

"Good evening, sir. May I take your phones? If you have any." They both handed them over, and they were then placed into a small box and then the box was given back to Simon so he could input a four-digit number and then given back to the person.

Now they were finally in the Richmond restaurant. The splendour was unbelievable. Summer could not believe her eyes. Politicians, movie stars, even football players, anybody that was famous was there. "Your table, sir, madame. Would madame like a glass of champagne?"

Summer said, "Please." Her body tingling with excitement.

"And, sir?"

"Yes, I'll have glass as well please."

The menu came with the champagne. Summer opened it to the first page, there were four pages in all and none of them had any prices on, but then why would there be. Summer glanced around the room trying to take in as much as she could, without being too obvious. The food was out of this world and the wine was fantastic as well. All in all, they both had a fantastic night but all good things have to come to an end and it was time to go. No bill came to the table as Charles said, "It's rude to show your money in a place like this.

The floor manager tapped Simon on the shoulder. "Sir, your driver is here. Shall I tell him to wait?"

"No," Simon said. "We are both ready to leave." Charles greeted them at the door and then they followed him to the people carrier picking their phones up on the way out. They were now in the people carrier. Charles asked if they needed anything else before he set off back to Hill Gate service station. "No, that's fine," Simon said as he sat back into his seat, his stomach full from the evening.

Summer asked, "Why can't you just drop us off at home? You could just drop us off at the bottom of the road."

Charles explained, "I would like nothing more than to take you straight home but I have been told to take you back to the service station where the taxi is waiting to take you home." Summer looked back out of the rear window at the Richmond as it faded into the distance and she realised she'd never get to sit at one of their tables again. Charles asked, "How did your evening go?"

Simon said, "It was okay."

And then, Summer interrupted, "It was fantastic. The place was an experience and it's something I'll never get to experience again, not in my lifetime."

Charles looked into his rear view mirror. "So you like the finer things in life?"

"Don't we all," Summer said.

Charles then said something that shocked Simon, "You have a pick up on Friday."

Simon said, "Yes but how do you know that?"

"It's okay, it was arranged by Teddy for you and Summer to meet him at The Fat Club."

"But how did he know Summer could make it? How did he know Summer wasn't working?"

Charles looked into the rear view mirror again. "Because you told the booking you could only do the morning collection as your wife was off for the day. Is that not so?" Simon looked in disbelief.

The evening was coming to an end. The people carrier pulled up behind the taxi that was waiting to take them home.

Charles said his goodbyes and closed the taxi door behind then.

Teddy was at home when his phone rang. "Good evening, sir." It was The Fat Club. "I have a Mr Chepstow on the line for you, sir. Would you like me to put him through?"

"Yes please. Ah, Charles, how did it go? Did my plan work?"

"Yes, sir. Hook, line and sinker. You now have Mrs Rodgers right where you need her. She's now had a taste for the high life and I feel she wants more."

"Good, then in your opinion, you think she'll come on board."

"Yes, sir, I do."

Teddy thanked Charles and said, "We will meet up for a drink in the future."

The taxi stopped outside their house. Summer got out of the cab first with her shoes in her hand, Simon was behind her as they both walked up to the front door. By this time, they were both giggling repeatedly like children. The drink had got a hold of them, they stayed up for most of the night. Summer just talked about everything they had just done then Simon said, "Well, you'll be able to thank Teddy in person on Friday when we see him."

Summer liked that idea, gone was the hate she had towards him, she was more inquisitive about him now. "What's The Fat Club like? Is it all high tech?"

"No, not really," Simon said. "It's just an industrial unit out in the middle of nowhere. He came back into the front room from the kitchen with another two glasses of wine, only to find Summer fast asleep on the couch, and rather than trying to wake her up and then get her upstairs to bed, he decided to put a throw over her. Thursday morning soon came around. Simon was up early, even though he wasn't at the car leasing company till one in the afternoon. He opened the door to the living room only to find Summer in the same place as he left her. He brought her a cup of tea and sat next to her. All that champagne hadn't done her any favours.

It was ten o'clock in the morning when Teddy's office phone rang. "Yes, Rose."

"Mr Triton and Mr Edhog are here to see you, sir."

"Thank you, Rose. You may send them up."

A short time later, the lift door to Teddy's office opened. "Ah, good morning, gentleman. Please come and sit down."

They both said good morning sir as they did so.

"Right then," Teddy took control. "What do you have for me?"

Oliver started the conversation, and every now and then, Jack would say his piece. "We have down loaded and deciphered the microchip that was on Youssef's name badge. First of all, he says he's still safe and is still okay to carry on…"

Teddy broke in on the conversation, "Are you sure that's what he said? Only the last message from him he was convinced his cover would be blown soon."

Jack checked his findings. "No, sir, he's now saying he's safe to continue."

"Carry on."

"Youssef has reported that there will be several organisations meeting in Rhodes with Mr Slimm chairing the meeting. At this moment, we think there's four organisations but we're not sure."

Teddy leaned back on his chair and folded his arms. "So you think it would be possible to get a man in on this meeting?"

Oliver looked at him and then turned to Jack. "I suppose so, but who were you thinking of?"

Teddy leaned forward. "Mr Bay."

"Mr Bay? But he's in prison, is he not?"

"Yes, he is," Teddy said. There was silence, an uncomfortable silence.

"Well, is it something we can do?" Oliver pulled his chair up the table.

"Yes," he said. "It's something we can do."

"Tell me how?"

"Well, we could alter the database slightly but I would have to have a word with our American friends as they use the same database, and I'm quite certain they will oblige for two reasons. Firstly, the four organisations that we'll be in attendance, one of which is from their country and they've been after this person for quite some time, and secondly, they owe us a favour for a product we got rid of for them in Brussels. They found the product dead in his bedroom the following morning."

"Ah, yes, that's right," Teddy said. "I remember Simon picked up Sinclair Robyn and took him to the airport. That was the day Sinclair gave Simon the run down on the Kite. Little did Simon know that was the business Mr Robyn was going over for." Oliver and jack looked at the documents just to make sure it could be done.

Oliver then looked up at Teddy. "We could put it into place but it would only last for two weeks and then who ever you're sending over would then be out on his own."

"Two weeks is all we need," Jack then said the only thing. "We can see there being a problem with is that the Americans will want Mr Slimm."

Teddy once again leaned back into his seat. "That's not a problem. With Mr Slimm out of the way, the organisation would fight amongst themselves and it could take years to rebuild. Right, gentlemen, make this work and you both could go a long way in The Fat Club. Are we clear? Oliver and Jack got up from their seats. Teddy rang down to Rose, "They're on their way down to you."

Simon was in his own meeting and it was a far cry from what Teddy had just organised. Simon was picking carpets for the car, and any other bits and bats that his drivers had asked for. Summer was sat in the back garden with her designer sunglasses on, nursing a very bad headache, the sort you get with expensive champagne and wine. Little did they know what was ahead of them.

Friday morning was here. Summer was feeling better, it helped that she stayed on Orange Juice the night before. Simon's coffee maker was gurgling in the background. They were both ready for the off and both feeling a little on the nervous side, and somewhat apprehensive. Summer was all for this as she told Simon repeatedly, but now the day was here, she wasn't sure.

The morning was a pleasant one and the drive over to Cumnor was as it always was. Summer didn't say a lot and when she did, there was a nervousness in her voice. Simon tried to make light-hearted humour but it didn't go his way. "Here we are, Summer, we're here."

Summer looked at him. "Is this it? It doesn't look much."

"Wait and see," Simon said as he opened the door for her. Now it was his turn to take a back seat as he had seen all of this before. Simon opened the door to reception. Rose was sat at her desk.

"Good morning, can I help you?" Her guard was never down even though she had met Simon before.

"Good morning. It's Mr and Mrs Rodgers to see Teddy."

"Please take a seat." Summer was the one that was nervous now. Simon was more relaxed because he knew what was coming. "Sir, we have Mr and Mrs Rodgers in reception for you. Yes, right, sir. Would that be tea for three, sir?" Rose got up from her desk. "Would you like to follow me and I will take you to Teddy's office. Follow me please." Simon was watching Summer's reactions to what was going on around her. Rose put her finger on the small square plate on the door into the Warehouse. The door opened and then shut tight behind them. They followed Rose down one of the walkways to the other end of the warehouse. Simon hadn't really noticed Rose before, she was always sat at a desk or bringing Teddy his tea. She quick stepped down the walkway with Simon and Summer, hot on her heels. Her thick tweed skirts stayed rigid as she walked. Simon still couldn't help but think he had seen her somewhere before, he just couldn't put his finger on it. They got to the other end of the warehouse. Summer's eyes had been wandering all over the place, trying to take it all in when Rose turned round to see if they were still with her. She then turned back to the square plate on the wall next to one of the doors. Summer went for the obvious door as Simon pulled her back.

"No, Summer. It's this one." As Rose looked back at him through the reflection in the door, that was it. That's where he had seen her before, she was the lady in the Straight Line Air Conditioning van that looked through her side window at him when he was walking through the car park at the garage. The lift door opened as Rose moved to one side Simon and Summer entered, and within minutes, the doors opened again.

Teddy got up from his desk to welcome them. "Good morning, Simon, and this must be your lovely wife, Summer." He held out his hand. "Good morning, my name is Teddy. I'm sure Simon has told you all about me."

Summer said, "Yes, he has." Teddy pulled out a chair for her, Simon sat down next to her.

Teddy then walked back round to his own chair. "Well, isn't this nice." Silence filled the air in the room. "Right then, I think you're both wondering why your here today. I think Simon has an idea. Don't you, Simon?"

Simon looked at Summer he put his hand on her knee to reassure her. "You don't have to go through with this, Summer. You can just say no."

Teddy interrupted, "Yes, you can, and at any point, you can get up and walk out of my office."

Summer put her back into the chair she was sitting on. "Go on then, tell me what's going on."

Teddy looked over at the lift door. "Where's Rose with that tea?" He really needed it now, he pulled the file from the side in front of him and then placed his hands on top of it. "Do you know a Mr Slimm? Have you ever heard of him?"

Summer said, "No, why should I know him."

Simon put his hand on her knee again. "Okay," Teddy said. "Let's start from the beginning. I think that's the best place to start, don't you?"

"I'm all ears," Summer said.

Teddy opened his file just as the lift door opened and in came Rose with the tea, she placed it next to Teddy's desk and then left the office. "So let's start from the beginning. You

both know about Mr Bay. This is very important for you, Summer, because we the Fat Club want you to work alongside your husband who will take the roll as Mr Bay, and you will be Mr Bay's wife. So let me now explain what we would like and how we are going to do it, and then you can tell me what you think. First of all, you know Mr Bay is in prison so what we're going to do, and it's being done as we speak. We have a team that is altering the prison database, so that will give you the time to do what the Fat Club needs you to do." Summer looked at Simon and didn't say a word. "Summer, you will take on the role as Julieta Bay. Her father's died and her mother lives in Argentina. Julieta moved back there in fear of any repercussions if she had stayed in the United Kingdom. The language barrier isn't a problem as Julieta spoke perfectly good English. Simon, you already know more then we can really tell you about Mr Bay, although there are a few small things we need to go through. Any questions so far?"

Summer asked, "What is it you've got us doing? Remember what you did to my husband?"

Teddy put his hands back on the file that was in front of him. The time wasn't right to open the file, yet, he needed to have them both on board. "Have you any questions, Simon?" He was curious and now eager to know what Teddy had planned. Teddy then explained that, of course, they both would be living the lifestyle of Mr Bay and his wife, Julieta, whilst in Rhodes, and would mean everything from their clothes to the six star hotel they both be staying in for the two weeks. Summer took a deep breath and then held it and then breathed out slowly to control her excitement. Teddy at last knew she was now on the end of his hook, all he had to do now was to reel her in.

The games afoot, a well-known phrase that Teddy use to say under his breath when he knew he had someone on his hook. "Would you both like me to open the file that I have in front of me?"

Simon was just about to say something when Summer once again jumped in and said, "Go on then." This was the person who said to Simon, 'Don't say yes to anything, you

know what you're like for getting involved with things that don't concern you.' He turned to her in astonishment.

"Look where we are now." Teddy opened the file to the first of five pages.

"Our man Youssef got some information out to us via yourselves, and this is very important and crucial to the Fat Club. Our American friends are also involved in this operation and will be assisting you, so it's imperative that we get this right. Simon, we, the Fat Club, decided that you would be the best person to send in because of your knowledge of Mr Bay and what better way than for you both go in as a couple. After all, you are husband and wife. Our agents would not get away with that." Teddy took one of the pages from the file and passed it over to Summer.

She gasped again, and held the sheet of paper close to her and then said, "You're kidding, tell me, you're kidding." Simon took it from her and looked at the now crumpled piece of paper. It was a list of their wardrobe consisting of high-end designer clothes, expensive watches, shoes and luggage for the two weeks they would be away. Summer snatched the paper back from him to have another look.

Teddy was now looking at page three. "Let me tell you a little bit about Julieta Bay. As you know, Simon, she went back to Argentina in fear of repercussions from any of her gang leaders."

Summer jumped in, "How can I pass off as her if she's from Argentina? That will be impossible for me to do." Teddy reassured her through Simon. "As I said before and Simon will tell you, Julieta spoke excellent English so there's no accent to learn. She was absolutely besotted by her husband and liked the finer things in life so, therefore, you both will fit in nicely."

Summer said, "This is all well and good but how dangerous is it going to be? I nearly lost my husband once before remember, so tell me how dangerous is it?"

Teddy pulled page four from his file and held it up in front of him with the text facing Simon and Summer. "I am not hiding anything from you both, it will all be explained to you

both later." Teddy put the page back into the file, and then waited.

Summer looked at Simon, he said, "Now you know how easy it was to get hooked last time."

Summer then looked back at Teddy. "Okay then, when do we go?"

"You both will go in three weeks. This is the date when Mr Slimm will be arriving there and if you decide to go ahead with this, then it will give us enough time to get you both up to speed."

Summer took hold of Simon's hand for some reassurance. He looked her in the eyes to calm her doubts or fears and then said, "It's down to you, but whatever you decide, you will have my backing all the way."

Summer looked back at him and looked at Teddy. "Okay then, let's do it."

"Good," Teddy said as he picked up his phone. "Rose, can you bring in the paperwork please?" It was only a matter of minutes as Rose walked into Teddy's office. She placed the paperwork on the left hand side of Teddy's desk and then stepped back. "Right, you know what this is, don't you, Simon?" He nodded his head as he looked at Summer. Teddy then concentrated on Summer.

"This document is the official secrets act, and as Simon already knows, it is a criminal offence to disclose any official information without lawful authority so you both must not, and I repeat, you must not tell anyone what you are doing. Do you understand?" Simon looked at him sheepishly and then put his head down. Teddy then got his pen from his top pocket. "Right then, if we're both happy, shall we sign?" He started to explained whilst they were signing the papers. "We're now going to get you down to London by train and book you into a hotel for three nights. There you will have personal shoppers that will advise you on what would be appropriate to wear. Do not worry about the cost, the Fat Club will look after it." Teddy continue to say, "Your items will then be put to one side ready for your trip. On the day of your departure, we will arrange a pick up. Again, it will be away

from your house, and all your luggage will be waiting for you both with more information about Mr Slimm and what we The Fat Club need you both to do, and that's all for today." Teddy then asked Rose to take them both to reception where Simon and Summer made their way back to the car, and then just sat there looking at each other, where Simon said,

"OH NO, NOT AGAIN!"
THE END